Dangerous Ties

Dangerous Ties

By

Debra Parmley

Debra Parmley

Other Books by Debra Parmley

Aboard the Wishing Star
Trapping the Butterfly

Desert Breeze Publishing, Inc.
27305 W. Live Oak Rd #424
Castaic, CA 91384

http://www.DesertBreezePublishing.com

Copyright © 2012 by Debra Parmley
ISBN 10: 1-61252-921-6
ISBN 13: 978-1-61252-921-9

Published in the United States of America
eBook Publish Date: February 15, 2012
Print Publish Date: April 2013

Editor-In-Chief: Gail R. Delaney
Editor: JD Lux
Marketing Director: Jenifer Ranieri
Cover Artist: JL Fuller

Cover Art Copyright by Desert Breeze Publishing, Inc © 2011

All rights reserved. No portion of this book may be reproduced or transmitted in any form or by any electronic or mechanical means, including photocopying, recording or by any information retrieval and storage system without permission of the publisher.

Names, characters and incidents depicted in this book are products of the author's imagination, or are used in a fictitious situation. Any resemblances to actual events, locations, organizations, incidents or persons – living or dead – are coincidental and beyond the intent of the author.

Dedication

To Mike, my husband and "patron of the arts", for supporting this artist and making it possible to follow this dream.

Thank you to my family for their unfailing support.

Special thanks to Charles Welshans and Aubrey Stephens my gun gurus, for critiquing the gun scenes. Learning to shoot a black powder gun in the deep south in the heat of summer was invaluable to understanding what a shoot out must have been like. Thank you to Cliff EaseleyEasley for providing a place to shoot and to Aubrey and Cliff for the lesson.

Thank you to Gail R. Delaney, editor-in-chief of Desert Breeze Publishing, my editor JD Lux, marketing director Jenifer Ranieri, my cover artist J L Fuller and the entire Desert Breeze Publishing family for their hard work and dedication to the quality of this book.

Special thanks to Gail R. Delaney for allowing me to expand this story from the original eBook version for the print version. Readers wanted to know more about Lillian and Nick and I'm pleased to be about to share more of their story. A special thank you to Valentina Taran for being my first reader and copy editor of this expanded version.

Chapter One

Nevada 1860, part of the Utah Territory

Pain erased all sense of time. Lillian didn't know how long she'd hung, her muscles exhausted from the strain, her mind full of warnings she was helpless to do anything about.

Her throat was raw from screaming before Grady had gagged her. Now the cloth gag stuck to her dry tongue. She squinted through tired eyes at the pail of water sitting by the edge of the mineshaft. She could look right down into it, the water taunting her with how good it looked, how it would taste cool and refreshing as it slid over her tongue, down her throat. It would soothe her throat if she could just reach it.

But there was no hope of that.

They'd tied her up and left her to die of thirst. Lillian closed her eyes.

No, don't look at it. Don't think of it. Think of something else.

Pain shot from her broken right toe up her ankle and leg. The scent of burnt flesh still filled her nostrils. He'd seared the brand across the top of her breast. Memory lodged in her body where pain radiated along with heat, echoes of his laughter still ringing in her ears.

A single tear slipped out and ran down her cheek.

It hadn't mattered what he did to her or how relentless they were. She still couldn't tell them where the money was. She couldn't tell because she didn't know. And no amount of torture could change that one fact.

Lillian squeezed her eyes tight and prayed her lie had bought enough time to get away. Though how she'd ever get out of this she didn't know.

She had to get away before he returned, angrier than ever because she'd lied.

Mr. Thomas Shelton, her former fiancé, was probably well to California by now, and rich as the cream Lillian used to pour into her tea every afternoon. He'd done more than abandon her along with the promises he'd made to her. He'd left her to face the anger of everyone in town who he had robbed.

Dear God, but she was thirsty. If she could only have a drop or two of water. Lillian kept her eyes closed so as not to look at the pail again.

Mr. Shelton, the president of Shelton Security Bank and a widower, had finally asked for her hand in marriage after months of waiting. She'd thought she'd close the dressmakers shop. Fact was, she wasn't making much money. It hadn't been going well. The women living in town or in the outlying areas did their own sewing and except for a few bridal gowns and mending the saloon women's clothing, Lillian had made no other sales. The Utah Territory was nothing like New York, where a woman needed a new gown for an event or wanted one simply because it was the latest new fashion.

She'd been foolish to follow her cousin out west, even if he was her only living relative. Carl was nothing like the boy she'd grown up with. Letters could be so deceiving and she hadn't seen him since he was ten.

Yet he'd written to her, urging her to come out west after her parents died. Convinced her it was better to be with family. Promised to help her set up a dressmakers shop now that she had to make a living. She'd always enjoyed sewing for herself and her ailing mother and the dresses she made always brought compliments.

She'd also been drawn in by the adventure of moving west. So she'd left the town she'd spent her entire life in.

Carl had been nice enough at first, helping her set up shop, introducing the townsfolk to her. But after the first few weeks, he spent all his time playing cards and running up debts in the saloon and the mercantile, then expected her to pay for them.

He seemed to have the idea that because he'd done this favor for her, she was indebted to him for life. It was a debt she could never repay.

Carl thought she owed him and he thought she had the money. Even her own cousin didn't believe her.

The pain in Lillian's shoulders from the pressure of her own weight pulling her down pushed away her thoughts. Her arms being stretched for so long made her jerk and flinch, though she knew it was futile to fight and she barely had any fight left. But she couldn't help pulling against the ropes even though it only made things worse.

Oh, what she'd give for someone to cut her down and a fast horse. She'd learn to ride, as if her life depended on it.

*****

Nick's horse made her way carefully down the mountain, his pack horse following along behind.

He wasn't far from town, and looking forward to a warm bath to wash away the dust of the trip and then a good hot meal. Maybe if he were lucky there'd be a warm and willing woman too. He'd been a long time without a woman.

It was then he saw her. Long golden hair, which caught the rays of the setting sun, lighting those tresses up like a flame. Red-gold hair swinging in a gust of wind.

What the hell?

He blinked twice to clear his head, in case he was seeing some fools gold of a dream.

But when he opened his eyes she was still there, bound by her wrists, suspended over a wide mineshaft; her bare feet tied together at the ankles and her long hair blowing in the wind.

Who had strung her up and why?

He pulled his rifle out and rode closer, his senses on alert. The area appeared to have been abandoned, but he knew you could never trust appearances.

The appaloosa lost her footing briefly and rocks rumbled down the mountain. He tensed, waiting for a sound or for the end of a rifle to appear, but all was silent and still.

He slowly rode closer. The only sounds on the mountain were the wind and the steadier footsteps of his horse.

By the time he reached the woman it was clear there was no one else about.

He swallowed hard, shifted in the saddle as his thoughts shifted.

Damn, she's beautiful. The knots are all wrong. Whoever tied her was no cowboy. If she struggles those knots will only tighten more, hurting her worse.

His fist tightened around the reins.

That's no way to treat a woman.

Her long hair blew in the breeze again. He rode around to the other side. He had yet to see her face.

*****

She heard horses through her dizziness, through a haze of pain. The horses' hooves steadily clopped closer and closer, bringing God only knew what. Her heart began to race.

Dear God, not them again. Please don't let it be them. Not again. I can't take much more. I don't want to die here, today.

The horses stopped and the only other sound was the wind. She could feel eyes upon her.

She didn't want to look, didn't want to open her eyes for fear of what she'd see.

But she forced herself to open them, fought the fear and the dizziness and for one brief moment her gaze met his.

Long enough to see his eyes were like summer lightning, intense and flashing with some dark emotion.

Then her world went black.

*****

Nick frowned when he saw the brand upon her breast.

Her blouse was torn, ripped down the side, exposing pale creamy skin so fair it clearly had never seen the sun. Newly drawn, in the shape of a curving "S" the scorched and bloody "S" was an abomination upon her breast, her skin.

The violence of such brutal torture hit him in the gut, taking him by surprise for he was not a soft man and he had seen much.

Who the hell had done this to her and why?

His gaze travelled up to the perfect oval of her face, eyelashes which rested against pale skin, golden hair trailing down unbound. Her pale cheeks streaked with tears.

They'd gagged her. She made no sound because she couldn't.

He clenched his fists. He wanted to hunt down the son of a bitch who'd done this to her and exact justice. He wanted to cut her down and take away the pain.

Her lashes fluttered and she opened her eyes to look straight at him, her eyes widening in alarm and pain. Fear flashed in her green eyes for one brief moment before she passed out completely limp.

"No. Damn it."

Rope burns marred her skin and the front of her skirt was ripped. Wind caught her skirt and it blew just enough for him to see the bruising on one leg.

He looked up at the rope, which was fraying above her bound wrists.

It wasn't going to hold. Need to get her down. Now.

"Son of a bitch."

That rope breaks and she'll fall to her death.

He gathered his lasso, looped it around and threw it once to test it.

One chance. It might be all she had.

With a sure and practiced hand he regrouped and tossed a second time, this time a smooth vertical loop swirling. As soon as the top of the lasso hit the front of her knees he angled it under her feet and up, tightening the lasso around her legs. He pulled the rope tight, held it taut, looped the rope around his saddle horn and pulled on the reins to signal his horse to back up. As a trained cow horse, she knew to pull back gently on the rope.

Slowly he pulled her closer watching each breakage of the rope suspending her as her skirt slowly rode up her body.

He dismounted and gentled his horse, patting her on the neck, reassuring her. Then taking hold of the rope tied to the woman's ankles, he eased up the rope, before reaching one hand underneath her knees and one hand behind the middle of her back to hold her. He was poised to pull her toward him, when suddenly the rope snapped.

Her sudden weight pulled her backwards as her body fell, the quick momentum nearly pulling him forward down into the mineshaft. He yanked her closer, to prevent the fall, pulling with all of his strength, his jaw clenched tight. Both of them fell flat on the ground with a thump.

Damn that was close. Too close.

He closed his eyes for a brief moment and blew out a breath. Whew.

She was dead weight on top of him, though she didn't weigh much. She was all softness and curves, her long blonde hair spilling over both of them. Her body felt limp and soft. He blew the silken strands that had fallen across his face away and inhaled her sweet scent.

The sweet intoxicating musk of her body overwhelmed. She was bare beneath her skirt. He didn't like the thought of what that implied. Of what might have been done to her.

Damn. Nick swallowed hard.

She's hurt and needs to be cared for.

He rolled her over, off of him and onto the ground, wondering just how badly she'd been hurt.

Then he stood looking down at her and clenched his fists, fighting for control of his anger.

Thunder rolled in the distance and darker clouds overhead threatened. Through his anger he barely noted the storm nearing.

His thoughts raced almost as fast as the quickly moving storm.

She was lucky to be alive. Lucky he'd come in time.

He wished he'd come sooner, before they'd tortured and branded her, but at least she was alive. Now he needed to hurry and move her before the storm moved in provided she wasn't too injured to be moved.

What exactly had been done to her before they suspended her over the mine, leaving her to her death?

He bent down next to her watching the way her chest rose as she breathed. Her bottom lip was split and swollen. Blood had dried there, in a dark red line. Controlling his anger before he touched her, he eyed the brand upon her breast again as he pulled the torn fabric of her blouse up to cover her.

The sight of the brand infuriated him and it was easier to care for her if he didn't have to look at it.

The thin cotton blouse she wore, though it was as torn and battered as she was, belonged to a modest woman. A lady. The pattern of light pink embroidered flowers across the white cloth was something a woman from back east would wear. Not something you could find here in the Utah Territory.

How had a woman from back east wound up way out here at a deserted mine shaft and in this condition?

Lightning flashed overhead illuminating her red gold tresses which reminded him of his first sight of her, dangling over the mine shaft, her hair bright as an angel who had descended to earth.

His anger flared brighter.

Who was the son of a bitch who'd done this to her? And why?

No woman deserved to be treated this way.

It made him madder than hell. He was angrier than he'd ever been in his life.

And he didn't even know her name.

Chapter Two

As she lay upon the ground, Nick worked loose the gag in her mouth. His jaw tightened at the sight of her swollen lip, blood seeping from where her lip was split as the movement of the gag cracked the dried blood open again and new blood seeped out. Her lips and mouth were dry, the gag dry as well.

He tossed the gag aside in disgust.

They hadn't given her water. Who knew how long she'd been here on the brink of death.

If the fall hadn't killed her, the lack of water would have.

Again he wondered who wanted her dead and why.

She was beautiful. Like an angel fallen out of the sky straight into his arms. Better treasure than anything he'd find in this abandoned mine. There was peacefulness to her features despite all she'd been through, yet he knew it was just her outer appearance.

Her beauty was a distraction, just like his anger and he didn't have time for either one right now.

Nick checked to be sure she was still breathing, her heartbeat strong, then let out a breath he hadn't known he held.

He bent down to work loose the rope, which wound tight about her wrists, but the knots in the rope were too tight. As he reached for his knife to cut them away, thunder rumbled closer overhead and he glanced up at the darkening sky.

Damn.

Those storm clouds had moved in fast. The sun was almost down then it would be dark.

He'd need to move her into shelter, away from this open area and this mineshaft, tend her wounds, wake her, and see if she could take food and water.

Though water was an immediate need, he also wondered how long it had been since she'd last eaten. He wondered how long she'd hung there before he'd found her.

Thunder rumbled again and raindrops came pouring out of the sky as he lifted her into his arms and carried her toward his horse. He laid her across the back of his horse then climbed along behind her. He gathered the reins and headed down the mountain. He tipped his head forward, using his hat brim to shield her from the rain as much as possible and headed for what appeared to be a shack.

A loud crack sounded overhead and the heavens opened. Rain drenched them both. He felt the warmth of her body slipping away beneath the cold rain and darkening skies.

By the time he reached the building she was drenched. He kicked open the door of the shed and glanced inside to be sure there were no unwelcome surprises.

The sky was dark. He made out little inside other than a few tools, the hard dirt floor and a broken chair. He carried her inside, laid her on the ground, and went back out to get his horse and packhorse to bring them in.

Whoever had done this to her might return.

He grasped Moonlight's reins and led her inside. "Looks like you'll have to sleep in the saddle tonight, girl." He loosened the saddle and patted her rump. "Can't take any chances."

Then he led the packhorse in and loosened her girth.

Nick glanced back at the woman. She'd not moved from where he'd placed her. He propped the door open with the broken chair to be able to see clearer. Taking off his long coat, he shook water from it and laid it beside her on the dirt floor, then removed his rifle and laid it nearby.

Going about his tasks he never lost sight of the woman.

Removing his bedroll, he unrolled it on top of his coat. Then he pulled a tin of ointment out of his saddlebags.

She was breathing slow and steady, the color in her face returning beneath the bruises.

Sliding his arms beneath her, he lifted her gently off the dirt floor and onto his bedroll, then eased his arms out from under her and sat back on his heels, watched her for a moment, his eyes adjusting to the darkness in the building.

When the lightning flashed outside it illuminated everything. The way her sodden blouse and skirt clung to her body, her wet hair and lashes, the moisture beaded across her skin. He swallowed hard, his mouth dry.

A woman like that should be treasured not branded like the cattle, bought and sold.

He wondered where her people were and how she'd come to be in such a state. He wondered why she seemed to have no one to protect her.

She needed to be cared for. And he wanted to care for her even though he didn't have time for this.

He bent down beside her and worked at the ropes binding her wrists.

They were tight. It would take his knife to cut through them. He reached for the large knife he wore in a pouch off of his belt and unsheathed it.

Cutting through the ropes, careful next to her tender skin, already marred by rope burns, he didn't want to cut her. The work seemed tedious and slow. More so because the ropes were tight and in the darkness he wanted to be sure not to hurt her any more than she was already.

Taking off his hat, he wiped his sweating brow. Humidity had been heightened by the storm. He placed his hat on the ground then turned back to his task.

Once he'd cut her wrists free, he laid the knife down and felt along her arms, one at a time, checking for broken bones. Feeling her soft skin beneath his fingertips, her small delicate bones made her seem fragile. She was lucky nothing was broken. He checked each shoulder to see if they'd been dislocated.

Nick placed her arms down at her sides, as gentle as he could, knowing they'd be painful and stiff when she awoke and not wanting to wake her yet. Then he moved to cut loose the knots about her ankles.

The more he examined her injuries, the more anger he felt toward whoever had done this to her.

Once her ankles were free he examined her legs, checking for broken bones. Nothing was broken, but bruises covered her body. As he'd suspected she'd been spared nothing. He blew out a breath of anger and exasperation and pulled her skirt together.

This was not the time to be angry. There was a time and place for that and he would deal with it when he dealt with whomever had done this to her. Right now, caring for her was most important. Answers and action would come later.

He'd need to remove her clothes and get her warm again. Get circulation and warmth back into her fingers and toes. Nick cut away the rest of her damp torn blouse with his knife. The spare shirt in his pack would cover her. It was much too large for her and he'd have to roll up the sleeves.

Reaching beneath her, he found the lacings to her skirt and loosened it, slipping it off down over her hips and past her legs until she was completely bare.

The sight set him back on his heels and made him catch his breath. Her beauty kept capturing his attention despite his efforts to focus on the tasks at hand.

His attention went back to her beautiful battered face. She needed a name so he wouldn't keep thinking of her as just "the woman."

"Angel." He whispered the name.

It was the first name that came to him. He didn't know her real name, but this would do, until he did.

Nick laid her on his coat and grabbed the spare shirt from his pack, covering her and hoping it would keep her warm while he tended to her. Then he hung what there was of her clothes to dry upon a nail, which jutted out from the wall.

He reached for the tin of ointment, opened it, bent down beside her and dipped one finger in. Then he lifted her right foot to apply the salve to the rope burns on her ankle.

Her muscles tensed suddenly underneath his fingertips and she jumped as if to pull away. Even while unconscious, she was afraid of him, though she did not know him.

It was possible she would now be afraid of all men after the way she had been treated. He'd known women that had happened to.

He hoped it wouldn't happen to her. It would be a shame. The last thing he wanted was for her to fear him.

Nick handled her foot as gently as he could, determined not to hurt her further than she was already.

Her foot was soft, uncallused, and her ankles delicate. He wondered where her shoes were. She wasn't used to going barefoot. That and the softness of her hands along with the clothing she'd worn, told him she was likely from back east.

He rubbed the ointment over her ankle, feeling the delicate bones beneath her skin as the darkness of the shack made him rely on his fingers to learn what he could of this angel.

Her scent was fresh rain and woman.

With a quick soft move he put down that ankle and lifting the other he continued.

From the rope burns on her ankles it was clear she'd fought. She had tried to get away.

It would only have made those knots tighten, exacerbating her pain.

Nick watched the way her lips parted as she breathed out. Subtle signs telling him the ointment was a comfort to her.

He smiled, pleased by that knowledge and the way she responded to his touch. With a light brush of his fingers, he applied the salve.

Her body tensed.

He paused waiting for her to relax again.

"Shh, Angel. You're safe here. Shh."

As he continued to smooth the salve on slowly, being very careful as he touched her skin with his fingertips, her body relaxed and her breathing slowed to an even pattern.

"Broken Angel," he said. "That's what you are." He continued smoothing the salve with a soft touch. "Fell straight into my arms, didn't you, Angel?"

A breathy sigh escaped from her lips.

He smiled in the darkness. "You surprised me, Angel."

She breathed in suddenly as if she were awake.

He paused again not wanting to startle her into waking until he was done. So she wouldn't wake in fear of a man she did not know touching her.

Finishing with the salve, he then took his water pouch and trickled a small amount of water into her mouth. Just enough to moisten her tongue and lips but not enough to cause her to choke.

Her tongue reached for it though she was still asleep, before her lips closed.

"Shh. Rest, Angel. Rest."

A different man might have simply taken advantage of her weakened state. But Nick was not that sort of man. At the moment what he wanted most was for her to be well again and to open her eyes and smile. He wanted to hear the sound of the voice, which had made those soft sighs. He wanted to know her name.

Chapter Three

Someone was smoothing something over her skin.

Soothing. Yes, please. Keep doing that. Feels good.

The medicine soothed as warm fingers brushed across her skin while a man's strong, gentle voice spoke.

He was speaking to someone called Angel. His tone had a degree of warmth and concern as his voice soothed her, wrapping around her like a warm blanket. She could stay here and listen to his voice forever, drinking in the comfort of it.

Not Angel. Lillian.

She wished he would speak to her the way he spoke to Angel.

His voice settled down into her subconscious, the way the healing salve sank slowly into her skin, easing the pain.

Wish someone would call me Angel like that.

His voice made her want to sleep. So tired, and he was taking care of everything.

Nice dream. Touch me. Yes.

His voice made her want to sigh.

She breathed out.

Rest, his voice commanded.

Yes, rest. Stay here in the dream. Where no one can hurt me.

She drifted away again.

*****

When she gave a soft moan Nick stilled, listening and waiting for her to wake and look at him. But she didn't wake, and so he again began his administrations.

A flash of lightning through the open door illuminated the perfect oval of her face, lashes which rested against pale skin, her wet hair framing her delicate features.

When he'd finished with the salve, he put the lid on, and wrapped his bedroll around her for warmth. He'd planned to lie down beside her and warm her with the heat of his body, but a sound outside caught his ear.

Instead he crouched near the door, gun in his hand, ready and listening as he reached for his rifle.

A rider was approaching fast.

*****

Carl rode up to the mine, wondering if his cousin was ready to talk yet. Wondering how long it would take him to get it out of her. Wondering just how grateful Lil would be to him for rescuing her after Grady had roughed her up.

"Lillian?" He started calling so she'd think he was looking for her. "Lillian."

Since it had started raining the clouds were covering the moon and stars making it harder to see. Carl squinted in the dark, trying to make her out but he was having trouble seeing.

"Damn it."

The moment he came close enough to see she was no longer suspended over the mine, he applied his quirk to his horse's flank to make the roan run faster. He raced up to the mine and reined in his horse.

"Lillian?"

Where the hell was she? Had his stupid cousin been wily enough to get away?

She'd had more fight in her than he'd even guessed.

It was then he saw the broken rope dangling over the mine. He rode his horse to the edge to look down into the black pit, but he still couldn't see a thing.

"Lillian? You down there?"

She had to be dead.

"Stupid bitch. Couldn't wait for someone to rescue her. Had to fight until the rope broke. Damn it all to hell. Now I'll never find the gold."

Whipping his horse with the quirk in fury, he raced away heading back to town.

He'd better tell B. T. right away. This was Grady's fault, for not securing her well enough to ensure she'd be there when he rode in to save her.

Now his plan was shot to hell. His stomach clenched.

B.T. wasn't going to like this.

*****

Lillian came awake.

The first thing she realized was that she was no longer strung up over a mineshaft. And for that there was a brief moment of relief, a sigh of release and the knowledge she would live.

The second thing she realized was that she was lying on the ground and wearing a man's shirt with a blanket to cover her. She was in a dark place she'd never been before. She caught her breath, her gaze darting to the tall man who was crouched with his back to her, a rifle propped on the wall beside him and a large silver gun in his hand.

She did not know him. Was he the man who'd arrived just before she'd blacked out? Had he saved her? Who was he and what did he want? Did he know about the gold? Was he after it and her too?

Tense, her eyes scanned the darkness. She was alone with him and he appeared to be watching something or someone outside. The coiled tension in his body was clear, even in the darkness.

Just as Lillian was determining what to do, she heard Carl's voice calling her.

What was her cousin doing here? Was he alone? Had he come to save her?

Lillian closed her eyes, feeling sick as his voice carried to the shed and she heard what he said.

Carl was part of it. He'd betrayed her. He only wanted the gold.

He wasn't here to rescue her and even if he was, his rescues came with too many strings. This severed the one string, which tied her to him.

Blood kin or not I am done with you, Carl.

Which meant she was alone in the world. But she was alive and she would survive.

The stranger had started to turn.

Lillian closed her eyes, calmed her breathing, pretending to be asleep.

She heard him lay his rifle down nearby and tried to judge how far it was and how fast she could reach it.

If I could just reach that rifle I could take his horse and ride so far none of them will ever find me.

Even if she didn't know how to ride, she'd learn fast.

She attempted to move, but her shoulders and arms were heavy and tired, with a slight tingling sensation. Like when her foot fell asleep sometimes when she would sit the wrong way on it. Then when she would try to stand her foot would feel a tingling as it came awake again.

Once she started to move, the feeling would come back. She didn't think they'd broken anything.

Maybe I won't be able to reach that gun, or if I reach it, even shoot it. But I have to try.

With that thought she lunged.

The stranger had placed his Navy Colt back in the holster, but he turned just as she reached for the rifle, her arms weak and shaking.

"Oh, no you don't." Quickly grasping both her wrists, he pushed her back down, one wrist on each side of her head.

She'd missed her chance.

Lillian struggled and wriggled beneath him, trying to get away, her eyes wide with fear.

He applied more pressure, forcing her to be still even as she winced from the rope burns on her wrists.

"Lie still." His voice rang with command.

She had no choice. He held her still, not moving, looking directly into her wide eyes, their noses just inches apart.

Those dark brown eyes. She'd seen them somewhere before, but where? She didn't know him.

She panted in fear as racing thoughts and emotions filled her mind.

"I'm not going to hurt you," he said.

Lillian wanted to run as fast as her heart was racing. She knew what he wanted. Why else would she be half-naked?

If he knew about the gold, he'd want it too. Or maybe he did. Maybe he wanted both.

The impact of his firm, but gentle grip and his forceful voice, his brown eyes steady and calm, stilled her. There was something in his eyes that told her he meant her no harm. Something familiar about them she could not place.

He was like a rock, unmovable.

He repeated the words. "I'm not going to hurt you." His calm, firm gaze riveted her, his dark insistent eyes reinforcing his words.

Words that were hard to believe.

"I'm not going to hurt you," he repeated.

That voice. She knew that voice. She hadn't dreamed it.

Angel. The name resonated in her memory.

One small part of her wanted to believe him. But she didn't dare. Lillian was done trusting men.

A man would promise anything, if it got him what he wanted.

Her skepticism must have shown in her face, because he blew out a breath. "Hell, I don't expect you to trust me." He regarded her for a moment. "Not yet. Not after what you've been through."

She tried to speak but could release no more than an unintelligible rasp. She frowned with frustration. The attempted lunge had worn her out and she couldn't stand feeling so weak and helpless when she still wanted to grab that rifle and run out the door. He wouldn't trust her now that he knew what she had in mind.

They both eyed each other in silence, gauging the other's reaction.

Finally he spoke. "You need water."

She nodded.

"All right. I'm going to release you now. Lie still and don't try anything stupid."

He let her loose and she slowly pulled the blanket back around to cover herself while he kept his expressionless gaze on her upper body. Then she laid still.

He nodded his approval. "Be still now. I'm going to get the canteen."

She didn't move or speak, but her wide eyes followed him as he went for his canteen.

He uncapped it and knelt beside her again.

"Here." He slipped one hand behind her head to help her sit up, and brought the canteen to her parched lips. "Sip it slow. I don't know how long you've been without water, but you'll need to take it slow."

He held the canteen and she took a sip.

Despite her thirst, Lillian drank slowly, watching the handsome stranger with caution.

His face was stern and almost expressionless, but for his eyes.

His eyes held intensity like none she'd ever looked into before.

This man was unlike any man she'd ever met. Strong, yet gentle. Stern, yet kind. And dangerous. Perhaps more dangerous because his softer side could deceive her. Oh, but that was the woman she was before. She was not so easy to deceive now. Even if he was the most handsome man she had ever seen. She was done being deceived by handsome men.

The way he'd handled his gun with such smooth movement suggested he knew how to use it quite well.

She'd seen a shootout right in the middle of town two days after she'd arrived. And this stranger was smoother than either of those two men, even though all she'd seen was him holstering his pistol before she'd lunged and he was on top of her. Onto her so quick she'd had no chance to reach his rifle.

Though weak as she was, she'd had no chance anyway.

She hated feeling weak and defenseless and at the mercy of a complete stranger.

His gaze upon her was steady and smoldering.

What did he want? Perhaps that was a foolish question. He wanted what every man wants. The question was how far would he go to get it?

Nick waited until she'd swallowed and then pulled the canteen away. "You can have more. But first, tell me your name."

"Lillian Hayes." Her voice croaked and she frowned at the sound of it.

"Nicholas Brace. Call me Nick."

"Lil."

"All right, Lil. More water?"

She nodded her head yes, her tongue still too dry to say more than a few words.

He held the canteen to her lips and watched her as she drank from it. "You were in bad shape when I found you. The rope wouldn't have held much longer."

"Yes, I know." She croaked out the words in a voice that didn't sound like her voice and her throat was still dry and sore. "Thank you."

"No need to thank me. You can however, tell me who strung you up over the mine and why."

She took several swallows before answering. When she had finally had enough water to speak more than a couple words she responded.

"Unless you're from around here you won't know who they are, even if I told you."

"If?" He pushed her back down with a firm hand. "There is no if. I saved your life. The least you can do is tell me who was trying to kill you and why."

"It's a long story."

"Well, Lillian. It's not like we'll be going anywhere in this storm tonight."

Thunder crashed and lightning flashed outside, emphasizing his point. She was stuck in here with him, who knew for how long?

Who knew how long it would be until B.T. sent his men back out to look for her? As if he'd read her thoughts he spoke again.

"I'd think it would be wise to tell me your story before whoever that was nosing around the mine shaft reaches the person he was racing off to see and they return to finish the job. Don't you?"

She covered her face with her hands. Her cousin would go straight to B.T. She was lucky to be alive this time.

B.T.'s men would surely kill her next time.

This stranger had saved her life. She did owe him an explanation of how she ended up branded and dangling over the mineshaft.

She gazed at Nick, wanting to tell him but having trouble finding the words.

Then, in the most compelling voice she'd ever heard, Nick said, "Tell me."

Chapter Four

Lillian took a deep breath and let it out with a sigh. Then she pulled her hands away and looked off into the corner as if she could see something off in the distance. Her voice came out as a low whisper.

He leaned closer in order to hear.

"Mr. Thomas Shelton, the president of Shelton Security Bank, took a shine to me as soon as I moved to town. We started keeping company, and a few months later, he asked me to marry him." She glanced down at her bare left hand and remembered how Carl had snuck the ring out of her jewelry box to pay part of his gambling debts after her finance left town. She'd taken the ring off unable to stand the sight of it. Yet the ring had been hers, not Carl's to take. "My fiancé made a lot of promises to a lot of people. Especially the people who deposited their gold in his bank for safekeeping."

She looked up at Nick and he handed her the canteen again. "Drink."

Lillian drank then cleared her throat. "The gold was in his safe, but not for long. And he was keeping it, but keeping it for himself." She shook her head. "I don't know what he did with the gold before he skipped town, but the bank notes he handed out aren't worth the paper they're printed on." She sipped from the canteen again.

"Sounds like you should be glad you didn't marry him." Nick frowned. "Is he the one who did this to you?"

She shook her head. "The men he tricked assumed that as his fiancé I knew where the gold was. But I never knew where it was and I don't know where it is now, or where he is either. He left town without telling me he was leaving. I've had nothing but bad luck since I met Mr. Thomas Shelton and I know I'm not the only one to feel that way. When the men found out he'd left town, they came after me."

"And that's why they strung you up over the mine?"

"Yes." She looked quickly away, clenching her fists as her voice shook. "They kept at me for days and when I couldn't tell them where the gold was, they hung me there and left me to die."

"And that's when I found you hanging over the mine."

"Yes." She wrapped the blanket tighter around her shoulders and hugged herself. "I thought you were one of them and had come back to finish me off."

"No. I was traveling through and saw you. Maybe your luck has changed for the better."

"Has it?" She looked skeptical.

"You're not dead. And for now they don't know where you are. I'd say that's an improvement. You're safe and we have food and water. Tomorrow I'll ride into town and find the sheriff. Those men will pay for what they did to you."

She frowned and shook her head no.

"Lillian, I'm sorry for what you've been through. No woman deserves to be treated like that, no matter what she's done. And it sounds as if you've done nothing wrong. Don't be afraid. I'll be with you. And I'll tell the sheriff how I found you."

"No." She shook her head adamantly. "B.T. is behind it, and the sheriff is a friend of his. Besides," she shrugged, "everyone in town is angry with me. No one will care about what they did to me."

"I think you're wrong about that," he said in a quiet sure voice.

"You don't understand. Even my own cousin..."

He frowned and leaned forward as her voice trailed away. "Go on... what about your cousin?"

"My cousin Carl was part of it. He's the one who rode back here to see if I was alive. Now he's gone racing back to town to tell B.T. I'm dead." Her voice cracked. "I didn't know he was in with them until he came here to look for me and I heard him talking. I thought he cared for me."

A single tear ran down her face.

He reached forward and though she flinched and eyed him warily he used his index finger and tenderly wiped her tear away.

"My own cousin finds out I'm dead and doesn't give a care. Other than to be angry because now I can't tell him where the gold is." She bent her head and her shoulders started to shake. "He was the only living relative I had.

Nicholas gave a nod. "You trusted him, but now you know how he really is."

There's not a man in the world I can trust.

She watched Nicholas Brace for a moment then nodded back at him. "Yes. Now I know. It's better to know."

Trusting men only leads to being hurt.

*****

Carl rode up to the saloon, leapt down from his horse, looped the reins over the hitching post and hurried inside. "Where's B.T.?"

Nob Li stopped drying off the glass he was holding and pointed upstairs.

"Damn it. This can't wait. He with a woman?"

Nob Li, shook his head no, his pigtail swinging behind his bald head.

Carl strode up the stairs, agitated as all get out.

At the top of the landing he called out, "B.T.?"

A door opened and B.T. stepped out into the hall. "Something wrong,

Carl?"

"Hell yeah, something is wrong. Damn fool of a woman fought the rope till it broke, that's what."

B.T.'s eyes narrowed to slits. "Keep your voice down, damn it."

Carl dropped his voice into a whispered hiss. "Now she's dead and we won't ever find that money."

"You see the body?"

"Didn't have to." He shook his head. "I saw the rope. The fall killed her sure as I'm standing here. And it was too dark and rainy to see down into the mine."

"You ever heard of a lantern?" B.T. turned away in disgust and muttered, "Incompetent." He headed down the stairs.

Carl followed along behind him, disgruntled at the insult.

B.T. stopped at the bottom of the stairs. "Nob Li?"

He raised his head and looked over at them.

B.T. gestured to him and he hurried over to join them.

"Come into my office, both of you." He glanced around the saloon, taking note of who was in the room. He waited until they entered his office and shut the door.

"Carl here says the woman fell into the mine and died. That right, Carl?"

"That's what I said."

"But he hasn't seen the body." B.T. gave Carl a peculiar look.

Carl knew in that moment that B.T. didn't trust him. B.T. thought he'd rescued his cousin as planned and was going to keep all the money for himself. And B.T. was not a man to cross. "Her body has to be at the bottom of the mine. The rope broke."

B.T. turned to Nob Li. "I want you to ride out to the mine. If you find the woman alive, bring her to me. And if you find her body," He reached into his desk and pulled out a pearl handled knife then slammed it on the table. "Cut off her hair, all of it." He laughed. "Till she's bald as you. And bring it to me."

Nob Li grabbed his pigtail and nodded. B.T. was always threatening to cut it off, if Nob Li failed him in some task or other. The Chinaman would follow his instructions to the letter without question.

Barely speaking English, there weren't many questions he could ask anyway.

B.T. reached under his vest and pulled out a shiny 32 caliber Colt. He held it out and said, "I'll want this one back."

What B.T. gave he often took back, as the mood struck him, and Nob Li was on a lesser rung than the other men, being a Chinaman.

Nob Li picked up the gun, then solemnly picked up the knife, the nub of his forefinger sticking out and tucked the knife into his clothing, out of sight before bowing silently out of the room.

"Carl, I'm inviting you to join the poker game tonight." B.T. pushed a piece of paper across the desk. "Sign. Play as long as you like."

And Carl knew it was neither an invitation nor a request. B.T. didn't want him out of his sight until he knew that Lil was dead.

"Where's Grady?"

"I gave him a job to do. He's far away from that mine."

Grady would do anything for the right price. Hell, he'd even volunteer if it involved beating or raping women. For one minute Carl wondered just exactly what had happened to his cousin, but he quickly brushed the thought away.

She was dead. No point feeling any guilt about it.

If she'd just held still he would have rescued her, they'd have the money and he could have taken her to California and started fresh.

B.T. waited for him to sign with a smile upon his face.

With a sinking feeling, Carl knew before the night was over, he'd be even more deeply indebted to B.T.

He reached for the pen and signed his name.

*****

Nick wasn't asleep; he'd needed to stay awake in case someone came along. He'd been too long without sleep and the rain outside made him drowsy. Once the sun rose, he'd get up and make coffee. See if there was dry wood to build a fire.

Lillian had fallen into an exhausted sleep and curled onto his shoulder as she slept, seeking the warmth of his body, something he suspected she would not have done while awake. She was still wary of him and her every movement and expression showed it. He'd wrapped his arm around her and held her as she slept.

She was soft and warm. It felt good to hold her. Too good.

He was so tired his eyes burned, so he closed them briefly and listened. He was still for a long time.

Just when he was in that place between sleep and wakefulness, he heard the rider.

He slipped away from Lillian, easing her head down upon the blanket, and moved to the door to look out.

The rider approached and got off his horse. Then he walked to the edge of the mine and stood there for a long time.

Nick frowned.

Damn. In the darkness the mine was too far to see what the man was doing.

He pulled out his gun before stepping out of the shack quiet so as not to draw attention to himself. Then he moved closer until he was close enough to see what the man was doing.

Bald with a long braid down to his waist he stood looking down into the mine.

Chinaman.

He'd taken a rope and lowered something into the mine. He stood craning his head this way and that then nodded once as if he was satisfied with whatever he was doing. Then he quickly pulled the rope back up and Nick saw it held a lantern.

Soon he would be done and turn to mount his horse again.

Nick returned to the shack and Lil, careful not to draw attention to himself.

As he stepped inside, a gust of wind caught the door and it banged.

Damn.

He turned, hoping it hadn't drawn the Chinaman's attention.

Watching as the man mounted and rode away he exhaled. Returning to Lil's side he slipped his arm around her.

Off in the distance a coyote howled.

Lil stirred and he held her close. "Shh, Angel. Everything is fine."

He stayed still, listening.

*****

Nob Li noticed movement out of the corner of his eye near the shack just before the door banged. He mounted his horse without looking at the shack and rode away as if he would not return.

Waiting until the sun was almost up, he made his way back to the shack, coming up behind it, his horse tied some distance away.

Someone was hiding in that shack. If it was the woman, he'd bring her back to B.T. Anyone else he would kill.

Chapter Five

Nick woke, instantly alert, sensing the man before he saw him, he drew his gun.
Then the shadow moved.
Knife.
A knife flashed in the dark.
Nick fired.
Lillian awoke with a cry.
The Chinaman fell backward against the door, holding his stomach and spouting angry unintelligible words into the smoke that filled the room.
"Nob Li!" Lillian turned, horrified toward Nick. "You shot Nob Li!"
"Shoot first, ask questions later." Nick stood, holding his gun on the wounded Chinaman, who was rapidly loosing blood from the hole in his stomach. Nick gestured to the knife, still clutched in Nob Li's hand. "You live longer that way."
Lillian coughed, waving the smoke away and wrapped her arms and the blanket around herself. The movement made her wince, as pain reminded her of the brand. She shivered at the sight of the knife Nob Lid held.
"He was going to kill us."
"Yes. I don't shoot a man without reason."
"You're not a gunfighter?"
A muscle in his jaw clenched. "No ma'am, I am not."
"Oh. Well you're very good with a gun."
"Thank you." He ground the words out.
Lillian wondered just who Nicholas Brace was. Despite the polite response he seemed angry with her.
He may not be an outlaw, but he handles his gun too well to be a simple farmer or preacher. He's dangerous with that gun and right now he is angry.
She wrapped the blanket tighter around herself, scooting back as far away as she could from them and watched both men warily.
This was the second time Nicholas Brace had saved her life.
Nick took a step toward the Chinaman, still holding the gun on him. "Who sent you?"
Oh God. If Nob Li came here to kill her that meant Carl had talked to B.T. When Nob Li doesn't return...
Nob Li gave Nick only a silent, blank expression.
"That wound is a bad one. You won't survive it. Might as well come

clean."

"He doesn't speak much English and even if he did, he won't tell you. He works for B.T. in the saloon. You see the nub where his finger should be?"

Nick glanced at it. "Yes."

"B.T. cut his finger off when Nob Li served him watered down whiskey by mistake."

"Harsh. So B.T. sent him here to make sure you were dead."

"Yes, but why would B.T. want me dead if he thinks I know where the gold is?"

Nick frowned. "It doesn't add up, unless he thinks your cousin knows where it is."

"My cousin, Carl."

"Yes. Whatever tale he carried back led to the Chinaman being sent here."

"I have no idea what Carl might have told them."

Nick nodded at the Chinaman. "That's a slow way to die."

He looked at Lillian. "See if he will talk to you."

Out of the corner of his eye, he saw Nob Li move, reaching for his gun. Nick fired.

Click. Click. Bang!

Nob Li, now slumped to one side, his eyes staring.

"Well, he's not going to tell us anything now. He's dead. We'd best move on."

"We should bury him," Lillian said. "Even if he did try to kill us."

"No time." Nick took the knife and the gun then pulled out a rope and tied the body to his horse.

"What are you going to do?"

"Drop him into the mine. Seems fitting."

Lillian had to admit the thought gave her a certain satisfaction.

"And it's the quickest way to hide the body."

Nick carried the body outside and over to the mine as Lillian watched. He stopped at the entrance to the mine and heaved the body in.

Watching Nob Li's body fall down into the mine, she blew out a breath of relief.

One down and three more to go. B.T. wasn't going to stop until he had the gold, so the only way to survive was to ride far away or to kill the men who were after her.

Three more men who'd try to take her life if they weren't stopped. Nick appeared to be just the man to stop them. Because he was very fast with that gun. If only she could hire him.

How did one hire a gunman?

It was impossible. Even if she knew how, she didn't have the money. Her fiancé had seen to that. Like everyone else in town, she was now broke.

She moved back inside and pulled on her torn skirt. It wasn't dry but she didn't have time to wait around and at least it was more clothing than she was wearing now. She hurried to dress then went back outside to see what Nick was doing.

Nick collected Nob Li's horse and looked him over before he started gathering his things. Finally, noting how silent she was he looked over at her and spoke. "I have business in town and thought you could go with me to talk to the sheriff, but this has changed everything. We need to clear out of here, fast and put some miles between you and anyone from town."

"I need to go back to town, get some decent clothing and close my shop if everything hasn't been stolen already."

"That isn't a good idea. It isn't safe for you." He shook his head. "If you go into town, they'll know you're still alive and you'll become an immediate target."

"Yes, but when Nob Li doesn't come back, B.T. will know something happened to him. And then he'll be back here, looking for me. When he doesn't find my body, he'll know I'm alive, so he'll find out either way."

"I'm not suggesting you stay here. That would be even more foolish. You'll come with me."

"Oh, I think not." She placed her hands on her hips.

He watched the movement with an amused smile.

"Lillian, you don't have a horse, water or food. You're wounded. And you don't have a weapon to defend yourself. Doesn't look to me like you have much choice, short of taking mine. And that is not going to happen."

Nick watched her process her thoughts. "This is what I have in mind. I have a herd of appaloosas I left back in the canyon north of here." He jerked his head over his shoulder. "While I was riding through I passed an abandoned house a little further north. You'll need a place to rest and heal. We can stay there until I decide what to do next."

It all sounds so reasonable when he puts it that way. So sensible.

So why did it rub her the wrong way?

She frowned. "Do you think they'll try to follow us?"

"Yes, if they can pick up a trail. I mean to see that they don't."

"And if they do?"

"You let me worry about that." He nodded and continued packing his gear.

There was something in the calm matter of fact way he spoke, something in his tone, which told Lillian she could trust him. But heading for an abandoned house with a man she did not know went against her upbringing and everything she had learned about men. It was a bad idea. But staying here would be much worse.

"I never learned how to ride a horse."

"So you're a city gal from back east." He nodded as if he'd already figured that out.

"Yes."

"Here. Let me help you." Nick held out his hand and she placed her hand in his so he could help her up onto his horse. He bent down on one knee. "Step up onto me."

His leg felt warm beneath the sole of her bare foot and she could feel the muscles of his thigh, hard and strong beneath her.

"Now, grasp the saddle horn and swing one leg over."

Her torn skirt wouldn't stay together and she fussed with it unable to relax enough to mount the horse even though Nick averted his gaze.

"Come on, Lillian. Get up on that horse." His tone told her he was growing impatient.

Finally she was up, seated higher than she ever had been before. The brand on her breast was stinging with pain and her limbs were shaky. She adjusted her torn skirt, attempting to cover her legs as her hand shook. She was unsure what to do next or why she felt so shaky.

"Just hold on for a minute and wait while I get Nob Li's horse."

"Hold on where?"

"The saddle horn or her mane. Oh, and Lillian? Don't worry about your skirt. I'm not looking and there's no one else around. Relax."

Nob Li's horse was testy and nervous. Nick spoke quietly and Lillian watched as man and horse eyed each other, sizing the other up. Finally Nick decided to tie the horse to his mount and Lillian realized they'd be riding together.

She wasn't sure what made her more nervous, riding a horse by herself when she'd never learned how or riding so closely behind Nick.

It wasn't long before they were riding away from the mine where she'd almost died, her arms wrapped around his waist, her bare feet and legs hanging down. She wished she had shoes or boots and a long riding skirt. But there was no one to see her and soon she began to relax.

The mine was out of sight and she focused on the trees and rode ahead, pushing the images from her time at the mine out of her mind, trying to forget.

I hope to never see that place again.

But it isn't over yet. I've only bought some time. They'll be after me soon enough.

A shiver ran down her spine with the thought.

It wasn't long until Nick realized she was shivering. He placed one hand on her arm and gave her arm a squeeze. "You're safe now, Lillian. I've got you."

They rode on in silence.

*****

B.T. was having a late breakfast of bacon and eggs when Grady informed him Nob Li hadn't returned.

"Hell, it's almost noon. He should have been back long before now."

He gave Carl a puzzled frown.

"You know I been here all night."

"I don't like this." B.T. poked at the eggs, which were now growing cold and then pointed his fork at Grady. "You ride out to the mine and see what you can find out. Hell, I should have sent you in the first place."

He'd sent Grady to pick up the trail Mr. Shelton had left. But Shelton had bought train tickets to four different cities. B.T. didn't have enough men to chase all the trains.

"You know what to do." He shoved his plate away and threw his napkin down in disgust as he left the room.

Grady left for the mine, a full days ride.

That evening when Grady returned he headed straight to B.T.'s office. Carl followed, closing the door behind them.

B.T. stood behind his desk. "Well?"

"Nob Li is dead and his horse is gone." Grady leaned over a spittoon and spat.

"You sure he's dead? You've seen the body?"

"Yeah he's down there."

"Damn it all to hell." B.T. glared at Carl. "And the woman?"

"The mine is deserted. But she stayed in that shed not long ago. I found blonde hairs and there's blood on the floor. Probably Nob Li's. And she's with someone."

"They leave a trail?"

"I wouldn't be standing here if they had. Whoever she's with cleared it and the rain took care of the rest. They could be anywhere."

"Damn it! I want that woman found." B.T. slammed his fist on his desk and glared at Carl.

"It ain't my fault. The rope broke and I didn't tie them knots or make the rope break. I want her found same as you," Carl said.

"Grady?"

"Rope was like he said. But someone helped her. She'd be dead if they hadn't. Some fool tied her with rotten rope."

B.T.'s eyes narrowed and he watched Carl. "You know who she's with?"

"No idea. She only had eyes for Shelton."

"Go through her place again. Maybe one of my men overlooked something. And Grady?"

"Yes, sir."

"When you find them, don't leave any loose ends. I want that gold and I want this cleaned up, fast."

Carl had a sick feeling in his stomach. From the look on B.T.'s face, he was one of the things B.T. might want cleaned up. He already knew too much.

"We need to find her." Carl put his hand on the doorknob. "She knows where the money is, I swear."

If he didn't find her soon, she'd collect that gold and be gone.

"You're not going anywhere. Grady will take care of it."

Carl's hand dropped away from the doorknob.

Grady nodded at B.T. and gave Carl a look as he headed out the door.

Carl had thought if he could find Lil and the money, everything could still work out the way he'd planned. But there was no chance to search for her if B.T. wouldn't let him out of sight. There'd be no chance to slip away.

Carl went into the saloon and rejoined the card game. He ordered a bottle of whiskey. If he couldn't leave, he might as well have another drink and enjoy himself.

But the cards weren't favoring him. He lost game after game.

He ran a hand through his hair and swallowed back another shot of whiskey, fast, then slammed the glass down hard.

B.T. scowled at him from the other side of the room, but Carl couldn't help himself. He needed the gold and being stuck in this saloon was making him stir crazy. He turned back to the card game, knowing his voice was getting louder and louder, but no longer giving a damn.

It wasn't long until a slim hand touched his shoulder and Emma's sultry voice whispered in his ear, "B.T. suggested I ease your mind some."

Sure, B.T. wanted him upstairs and out of the way. Well he wasn't about to turn down a good thing. He followed Emma up the stairs while watching her backside sashay as she climbed.

Emma stopped at the top of the stairs and took his hand. "Come with me, sugar."

He followed her with a grin, knowing he'd owe for this one too, but at least she'd take his mind off things for a while.

Maybe by tomorrow his cousin would turn up with the gold. She owed him one. He was the one who'd nudged her and Shelton together in the first place. She'd have been well-off married to a banker.

*****

Lillian noted how Nick was constantly looking about, wary of anyone who might be following them.

They rode in silence.

Lillian was exhausted, but too nervous to fall asleep. The scenery passed before her tired eyes in a blur, everything blending together until they reached the abandoned cabin. She couldn't have told anyone how they got there. Nick rode like a man who knew his horse and the land well, moving as if he were a part of it. He'd covered their trail away from the mine and said the rain would cover the rest of it. The quiet confidence with which he spoke and carried himself told her he was a competent man.

Now Nick slowed his horse and they approached the cabin with caution, his rifle in hand, though it appeared no one was about.

"Wait here." He dismounted and walked to the cabin.

It was dusk and the shadows made Lillian nervous. She clung to the saddle, waiting.

Thunder and lightning threatened over her head and she jumped when a big boom came overhead. The horse moved skittishly and the headache, which had been building in her head, grew stronger.

Finally Nick gave the all clear and came back to help her down off the horse.

"Been a while since anyone has been here. Come on, I'll help you down." He reached his hands up.

"Thank you."

His hands settled around her waist and she held onto his shoulders as he lifted her down, his strong brown gaze taking her in. Her legs were stiff and her thighs and bottom sore. He released her and waited, watching her as she moved, taking in her every expression.

Lightning boomed again and she jumped before wrapping her arms around herself.

"There's nothing here to be afraid of Lillian. You can wait in the cabin while I find wood for the fire."

He moved to take his bedroll off the horse and she hesitated.

"Well, go on." He frowned at her. "It's bound to start pouring down any minute."

She frowned back at him, but didn't move.

The thought of staying alone in that cabin with a man she didn't know had her nerves on edge more than the thunderstorm moving in fast.

He took in her expression. "What has you worried? They aren't likely to find you here. The storm will make it hard for them to track, even if they knew what direction to take."

"I," she started to speak then closed her mouth.

"Out with it."

"I don't know anything about you." She said the words all in a rush.

"What do you want to know?" He turned back to his tasks, glancing over his head at the dark clouds and hurrying to unload his gear.

"Where are you from? And why were you riding past the mine?"

"I have a ranch in the Utah Territory."

"Utah Territory is pretty big."

"Yes, ma'am, it is."

She waited for him to answer her other question.

He handed her his bedroll. "Here. Carry that in for me if you would."

"Yes, of course." She held the bedroll waiting for his answer.
"One of your townsfolk contacted me about the horses I have for sale."
"I see."
"I was on my way to town with one of the horses for him to examine."
"Just one?"
"Yep. Horse trading can be dangerous business."
"You don't trust the man."
"Trust has to be earned."
"Yes it does."
I've been too quick to trust in the past. I can't make that mistake again.
Something in her tone made him stop and turn to her.
His brown eyes gazed into hers as if he sought something.
Her eyes searched his.
What sort of man was he?
A raindrop splatted on her forehead and she blinked.
"I'll answer any other questions you have after we're inside."
He handed her the canteen. "Finish that and I'll refill it. There's a stream nearby."
Good. That meant fresh water to drink and perhaps a way to wash.
She uncapped the canteen and drank the two swallows left.
The water didn't even begin to quench her thirst.
Cool fresh water. How good that sounds.
"Are you okay?"
Realizing she'd closed her eyes, she opened them again and pushed away the thought of how badly she wanted to soak in a tub, to scrub every bit of filth off of her. She pushed away thoughts of how thirsty she was.
"Yes."
More raindrops splatted upon them both.
"You'd better get on inside."
She stood hugging the bedroll. "I just need to know one thing."
"What is it?"
"I need to know how you got so fast with a gun."
"Plenty of practice."
That wasn't the answer she was looking for. She stood waiting.
He moved faster without looking at her. "My pa had a trading post up north of here. He wasn't fast enough with a gun. I vowed to do better."
"I'm sorry to hear about your father. Was it Indians?"
"Nope. White man. Called my father an Injun lover." He yanked at one of the straps and his mouth formed a thin line as he blinked once, hard.
"Oh. I'm so sorry." Lillian backed away. "I, I'll just take these things inside now." She bowed her head, turned and headed toward the cabin carrying the bedroll beneath the raindrops now falling down faster.
He was a rancher, not a gunman. Her assumption about him in the

shack had made him angry, but this time her assumption had caused him pain she had never intended.

She'd experienced harsh treatment because of other people's assumptions. Harsh treatment that had almost cost her life. The good townsfolk had allowed their anger to turn a blind eye to B.T. hauling her away to question and even the sheriff had done nothing to intervene.

Assumptions were dangerous things.

At the door of the cabin she glanced back at Nick as he hurried to take care of the horses in the pouring rain.

They were not off to a great start, even if she was less afraid of him now. She would try to make it up to him.

Inside, as Lillian's eyes adjusted to the dim light of the one room cabin, she made out one bed, an oil lamp over the chimney, a table with one chair, and an old, worn broom in the corner. The earthen floor was cool and damp beneath her feet from the recent rains and she wondered if the thatched roof leaked.

She unrolled the bedroll upon the bed.

Where will Nick sleep? Certainly neither of us should sleep on the cold dirt floor.

She stood staring at the bed.

I'll get no sleep at all.

Attempting to forget about the bed and sleeping arrangements, as well as the awkward feeling brought on by their conversation, she decided to sweep the cabin. Taking the broom, she realized it had mostly been used to clean the fireplace. She swept the fireplace out, removing cobwebs and mouse droppings, the sweeping movements making the wound on her breast hurt. For a time she had forgotten about the brand. But she was feeling it now.

The pain and heat of her wound were now impossible to ignore. Memories of the hot poker against her skin returned and she willed them away, attacking the dirt of the cabin as if it were an enemy. Nick's shirt and her torn skirt were damp and dirty as they clung to her.

She rolled the sleeves up again where they had fallen down and wished she could wash and put on clean clothes again. She was used to wearing pretty dresses of her own design, not men's shirts which were too large for her. If only she had one of her dresses here. Trying not to think of the dresses waiting for her in town, she focused again on cleaning.

In the corner of the fireplace she found a coin that had rolled in beneath the mess. She picked it up and turned it over in her palm, soot making her hand and fingers black.

A laugh carrying an underlying bitterness bubbled up from within.

Nick walked in with dry kindling.

"What is it, Lillian?"

Why do I feel so warm when he is near?

"I found a coin. This coin could be the only money I possess now." She sighed.

"Told you your luck had changed," Nick said. He placed the kindling in the fireplace. "That's one coin you didn't have an hour ago."

"Well," she polished it against her torn skirt. "It's enough for a new pair of stockings at least."

Her torn skirt showed too much leg. What must he think of her? If only she had one of her good dresses on and looked more like a lady.

She glanced up at him and smiled. "I want to thank you again for saving my life. Twice."

"It was…"

She interrupted. "Please don't say it was nothing."

"I won't." He hesitated for a moment then said, "You're welcome."

"And I apologize for the assumptions I made about you. I would like us to start over. I," she frowned and glanced away over his shoulder. "I know what it is to have people think the worst of you." She looked back at him. "It's a horrible thing."

"Apology accepted." He nodded and the look in his eyes told her that he understood.

They stood in silence as she gazed up into his deep brown eyes, which watched her with a quiet intensity. Her stomach did a little flip and she caught her breath.

Time seemed to stand still.

Her gaze took in the stubble upon his chin, which emphasized his strong jaw, his dark hair and eyes and contrasted with his lips. Lips which now curved up in a smile.

Realizing he was aware her gaze had dropped to his lips, her face heated and she took a step back and rubbed the back of her hand across her forehead.

"It is so warm in here."

Much too warm for a fire. How can he be thinking of building one now?

"You can have the bed." His voice rumbled in her ear, interrupting her thoughts. "I'm planning to sleep over here, near the fire."

"Won't you be too hot by the fire? We don't need a fire. This cabin is so warm already."

"No." He frowned. "It's not warm in here. There's a dampness and the rain will make that worse."

His voice sounded as if it came from a distance. She stared down at the coin in her hand.

"I have enough for stockings. And I will need a pair of shoes and a decent dress. I can hardly walk though town like this, even into the mercantile to purchase what I need. It isn't proper for a lady to dress like this."

Wearing his shirt and her torn skirt, people would assume the worst and it would just add to the ugly gossip about her. Those horrible assumptions that had nearly gotten her killed. Which still might.

She looked at Nick as a wave of dizziness hit her.

The heat inside the cabin must be making her dizzy. She leaned against the broom before placing it in the corner.

Nick gave her a strange look. "You won't have to. Try not to worry about that right now. "

"Everything is at my store. I'll need my pink and white dress, or the light blue one. Stockings, that's what I need. White stockings for my pink and white dress."

Nick's brow wrinkled but he didn't say anything before stepping out to get more wood for the fire.

Dizzy, she sat on the bed and closed her eyes again.

So tired.

She'd only lie down for a minute to rest until Nick came back, then she'd ask him where the stream was, to wash the soot off her hands.

Only for a minute.

Lillian wanted to sleep, but she couldn't because her head had started to pound.

Her energy had been drained by the ordeals she'd been through and it was as if the minute she reached the bed, her body collapsed. It reminded her of something her grandmother used to say to her mother. "If you don't slow down and rest, God will make you slow down."

She'd not had a moments rest in days and the stress had caught up with her.

Her body wanted nothing more than to sleep.

It didn't matter that the bed was less than soft and she would soon be alone with a man she barely knew beyond the fact he was a rancher and the son of a trader who'd been killed.

Nick. He'll think I'm not a lady, going around without stockings. Need to get stockings soon.

*****

Nick frowned as he looked for dry pieces of wood to stock the cabin, hurrying as the rain continued to pour down.

There was something wrong with Lillian.

She was sweating yet it wasn't hot in the cabin. And she was rambling about dresses and buying stockings when she had more important things to worry about. She hadn't appeared to hear him when he'd told her not to worry.

He'd thought for a moment she'd wanted him to kiss her, but brushed that thought aside when she stepped back and started rambling.

Had her ordeal done something to her mind? Her cheeks were mighty flushed.

He hoped she wasn't ill.

Chapter Six

The fire was too hot.

Lillian pushed the blanket down away from her body.

Strong cool hands pulled the blanket back up and a cool cloth was placed over her forehead as she looked up through sleepy eyes.

The tall, dark haired man with brown eyes sat beside her, a look of concern on his face.

Who was he?

The brand on her breast was on fire and her memory returned.

"No!" She turned her head side to side. "I can't tell you. Don't know. Don't know."

"Shhh." His hand cupped her cheek. "There's nothing to tell. You're safe here. Rest now. Sleep."

Her eyes drifted closed again.

"Hot, so hot," she murmured.

"I know, Angel. I know. Thirsty?"

She tried to wet her lips with her tongue.

Yes.

She didn't know if she'd spoken the word, but he held a canteen to her lips and allowed water to dribble in as her tongue found it and wetted her mouth.

"Can you drink?"

That voice. Heard it before. Where? Knew him.

"Angel, you asleep?"

Sleep. Yes. Want to sleep.

*****

Nick watched her for a response and when none came he stood, stretching his back. He'd step outside, get some fresh air, refill their water supply and check on the horses. She'd sleep for a while and he would hurry back.

He didn't like leaving her but he also couldn't stay cooped up in that cabin forever. She'd shown improvement over last night when the fever had raged.

Outside the night was clear, the stars bright in the sky. He wished he could share it with her. Wished he could see those green eyes gazing up at the stars instead of gazing up at him in the delirium of fever.

He was concerned about her wound, which had become infected. Bathing it and dressing it hadn't been possible at first, because the fever had struck and in her delirium she wouldn't let him touch her. He'd thought to tie her hands down just long enough to tend to her wound but the absolute terror of her screams had stopped him and he'd hurried to untie her, hating the fact he had caused her terror to emerge, bringing back the memories of her ordeal.

It had made him feel lower than a skunk.

She was defenseless and in need of his love and protection.

He focused on anything he could do to ease her fever and tend to her wound until he finally stopped kicking himself for causing her to be afraid. He was doing the best he could for her and hadn't stopped to think what having her wrists bound again would do.

He would not attempt to tie her again. Even though it would have been much easier for him to cleanse her wound, he would not be the cause of her anguish.

Though he was a patient man, this situation they were both in was sorely trying his.

Already he was behind schedule. He should be in town by now, meeting with the buyer for his horses, setting up a time for final delivery. But he couldn't leave her in the cabin alone in the state she was in. Not for long.

Nick hurried to finish his chores and returned to the cabin.

She was still sleeping.

He removed the cloth and placed his hand on her forehead.

Still feverish but the fever had come down some.

He began to bathe her body with the fresh water, being careful around her wound and trying not to wake her.

Strange how familiar he now was with her body. Her breasts, her belly, her thighs. The softness of her skin. Her scent. How different it was to be touching a woman in this way, caring for her with no hope of her returning any sort of favor. Caring for her while keeping his desires at bay.

Recklessly his hand moved to her face, cupping her cheek, his thumb ready to caress her bottom lip.

He longed to kiss her.

Her breath eased out between parted lips to touch his thumb.

No. It was out of the question.

He drew his hand back and it trembled slightly before he made a fist.

Control. That's what he needed. Control. Longing for her didn't do either of them any good and the last thing he would do was anything to hurt her. He would protect her, even if it meant protecting her from him.

He took a deep breath, released it and unclenched his fist.

Strange how quickly he'd grown attached to her. How worried he was about her. Yet he barely knew her.

*****

Lillian was on fire. The brutal branding had spread heat throughout her body and she twisted and turned to get away, but there was no release, no escape, and no hope of escape.

No, no. Make it stop. Please no more.

"No!" She cried out in her sleep and twisted away from him.

"Shh, Angel. Shh. Lie still. "

Then something cool was placed on her head, something cool moved down her body. The dream changed and she was being bathed. Bathed by a tall, dark haired man with brown eyes who was speaking to someone named Angel.

Lillian. Not Angel. Lillian.

The soothing touch, the feel of his fingers across her skin felt so good. Yes.

The fire began to fade as if washed away by the man's touch.

Wish he would call me Angel.

*****

She murmured in her sleep, "Wish he would call me Angel."

He smiled. Guess she liked that. He tucked the knowledge away to save for later and went back to cooling her body down with the wet cloth.

Finally her fever broke. She shivered.

Nick pulled the blanket over her again and rubbed her arms as her eyes slowly opened and looked up at him.

"I'm glad to see you are awake again Lillian. You had a fever."

"Who are you?" Her eyes widened. "Where am I?" Her gaze darted about the cabin.

"I'm Nick and you are safe here. They won't find you."

"Nick, oh yes. You saved me before the rope broke." She frowned harder trying to remember all that had happened. "I don't remember this place." She frowned at him in utter confusion.

"You've had a fever, Lillian. Sleep now. We can talk later."

He didn't tell her they'd repeated this conversation several times over the past several days or hint at how it had tried his patience when she couldn't even remember his name. He didn't remind her of her wound, or tell her how it had become infected and how he'd bathed her to get the fever down or how he'd washed and dressed her wound hoping to clear the infection. He didn't tell her how worried he'd been or how relieved he was now that the fever had broken. And because her eyes were now closed again as she slept, she did not see even a glimpse of this in his eyes.

It was just as well. Seeing her so vulnerable and in need of his care had brought out feelings in him he hadn't known he had. Nursing the sick hadn't been something he'd done before. As a single man he kept to himself and with no living relatives, no one had ever needed him this way before. His experiences with women had never lasted through the whole night and had been of a different kind of need.

Nick stood, stretched and then with one last look at her sleeping form, her face peaceful now as she slept, he went outside for fresh air and an escape from the emotions of the moment. From the way his heart had softened toward her.

He was not looking to get more entangled with Lillian than he already was. Already she'd roped his heart and he had no intention of allowing those ropes to tighten any further.

She'd showed a side of herself before the fever had taken over. A side of her he admired.

When she'd thought beyond herself to admit her assumptions were wrong, asked him for forgiveness and to start over, she had completely changed everything he had thought about her.

Instead of being caught up in all that had happened to her, focusing on herself, which most would have done and with good reason, she had taken responsibility for the words she'd spoken and thought of how they'd made him feel.

It had floored him. And in those moments that followed he'd reassessed everything he thought of her.

She was far from broken. She was a woman with a strong and loving spirit who thought about others.

Lillian Hayes was an amazing woman. He'd never met anyone like her. And if this was how she was after all she'd been through and on the brink of a fever, how amazing would she be when she was healthy and whole again?

How had any of the townspeople believed her capable of stealing their gold?

She was a good-hearted person, an unselfish person who thought about others. Lillian's problem was she trusted too easily and she'd had no one reliable to depend on.

At least she hadn't until now.

But he didn't want her to become too dependent on him. He'd make sure she knew how to defend herself with a gun and he'd set things to rights before he moved on.

Thoughts of Lillian had been with him all the way to the creek even though he'd stepped away from the cabin to clear his head.

Nick splashed fresh water on his face and refocused.

The danger point was gone, now that her fever had broken. Lillian had pulled through and would soon be well.

Soon he'd be able to deliver those horses and collect his money. If this delay hadn't soured the deal. In the meantime, he had to check on the horses and catch a few fish if they were going to eat. Supplies were now low.

*****

Lillian woke; rolled onto her side keeping the covers pulled up to her chin and watched Nick as he bent over the fish cooking in the fireplace. The scent stirred her hunger and she wondered when she'd last eaten. She watched him through slanted eyes, not wanting him to know she was awake yet. Her skirt and his shirt that she had worn lay draped across the back of the chair beside her bed.

When had he removed them? Surely she hadn't taken them off. She wouldn't have done that.

She remembered little after arriving at the cabin and wondered how long they'd been here and why she felt so weak. Then memories of being ill with fever, a blur of fitful dreams and Nick's calm voice came back to her as she became more awake.

He was whistling as he cooked, a low whistle to some tune she'd never heard. The sound was comforting in a homey kind of way. There was something about listening to a man's whistle that let you know everything was okay and safe, no danger in sight.

The way Nick moved and spoke was also reassuring. His voice had a way of reaching deep inside her, to touch a part of her she hadn't known existed. She wished she could hear his voice right now, but didn't want him to know she was awake and watching him. She allowed herself to relax and take in the sight of him, slowly, savoring each glance.

His Levis were stretched tight, and he looked so good in them that she was drawn to look at the muscles in his back, his legs, and his thighs.

There was something about the way he moved. He added a few pieces of wood to the fire. Then he stood and abruptly turned to face her, catching her gaze with his eyes.

She blushed and glanced down and to the side.

"Glad to see you awake and well again, Lillian."

The warmth in his voice was evident, his voice reaching in and wrapping around that part of her which then felt warm and settled.

"How are you feeling?"

"Much better, thank you."

"I'm glad to hear that."

With just a few long strides he was standing before her.

She rolled onto her back, holding onto the blanket with her fingers, a sudden shyness because of her nakedness beneath the blanket causing her to tuck her chin.

Placing one finger beneath her chin, he tilted it up, her face coming up to look at him. He cupped her chin tenderly in his warm hand and regarded her carefully, an easy smile playing at the corners of his mouth.

His fingers were warm and firm.

She offered him a small, shy smile, too shy to speak.

At the base of her throat her pulse beat and she felt as if her heart had risen up into her throat. She'd never felt so alive in her life.

All this from the mere touch of his hand. And all he was touching was her chin.

She swallowed hard.

He looked down into her eyes, his gaze gentle and reassuring.

"No reason to be shy." A slow smile spread across his face. "I had to cool you down to bring the fever down so I've seen every inch of you."

She blushed at the thought of him touching and seeing every inch of her. Even her fiancé hadn't seen that much of her and she'd planned to marry him. During their intimate times she'd always been partially clothed and the lights had been turned off.

But Nick had seen every inch of her, had bathed her.

The thought of him bathing her made her warm in a squirmish way and opened all sorts of questions in her mind.

"Well, I don't remember." She frowned her displeasure. "I wasn't awake when you saw me."

His thumb barely caressed her still bruised lip, creating a tingle. Her lips parted beneath his touch.

"No." Amusement flickered in the eyes that met hers. "You weren't." His thumb brushed across her lip the other way. "You were sleeping like an angel."

Her lips tingling from his touch, it was as if he drew the words out of her. "I dreamed about somebody talking to someone named Angel."

"It was no dream, Angel." His smile deepened, his eyes full of some indefinable emotion. "The somebody was me and the someone was you."

She smiled back at him. "I'm no angel."

"Who wants an angel, anyway?" He winked.

Something about what he'd said and the way he'd said it made her toes want to curl. Sent a longing all through her body, beginning in her belly. The warm squirmish feeling changed to a longing to be touched, to be kissed.

Still holding her chin, he brushed her lips again with his thumb. "Does this hurt?"

"No," she breathed out.

His touch was so far away from anything that hurt it made her forget momentarily that anything did.

"Good." He bent toward her, leaning in for a kiss.

She closed her eyes, longing for him to do just that.

She felt his lips first kiss her forehead, then the tip of her nose, then each of her closed eyelids with a reverence and finally satisfying the longing she had inside, his lips brushed against hers as he spoke.

"Angel."

His lips touched her like angel wings, soft and with reverence.

Her soft and bruised mouth opened slightly as she breathed his kiss in, caught up in the tenderness.

Then she kissed him back, the feelings inside beginning a slow flow out.

Never in her life had she felt such tenderness. A tear escaped and ran down her cheek.

He stopped, raising his mouth from hers and gazed into her eyes, studying her.

He brushed the tear away with his thumb, watching her.

"I've never known a man to be tender." She gave him a confused look. "What do you want from me?"

"Nothing, Angel. Not a thing." He stood but continued watching her.

He confused her. The situation they were in confused her. Nothing seemed clear any more and she didn't know what to do with that. The way this man treated her went against everything she knew of men and it was the unknown nature of what hovered here between them, which frightened her. For what if this was yet another trick? What if this wasn't real? She would fall and fall hard, breaking her heart into little bitty pieces.

"You don't believe me." His disappointment was clear.

She sat up in the bed, pulling the covers closer to herself.

"You have the advantage over me, sir."

He cut her off before she could protest further. "What gave you the idea that a man couldn't be tender?" He stepped away from her, putting distance between them. "There's many a man who cares for his horse out on the range with a tenderness that would likely surprise you."

"It would, as I've never seen it before." She had only his word for it.

Words were only words.

Some men would say anything if the timing suited them, to get what they wanted. Some men could look straight at you and lie without showing one bit of difference in their expression between the telling of a lie and the telling of a truth.

"Sorry to hear that, darlin'. That's a real shame. Sounds to me like you've been keeping company with the wrong men."

She gave a bitter laugh. "No doubt about it." Then she gave him a look. "But then you know that about me already. You know a lot about me. More than I know about you. You know my whole life's story and you know things I wouldn't have told anyone."

"I know you've been through more than any woman should have to endure."

"Yes."

She stared past him as her thoughts returned to her recent past and the brand, which was again shooting pain into her body.

He leaned one hand against the wall and turned partly away from her. The moment he'd begun to move, her gaze had returned to follow him and now she could see his profile, strong and solid in the flickering candlelight now that it had grown dark outside.

"I know you are honest and loyal. But your loyalty and trust were misplaced and because of that you've been wounded in more ways than one. And you have a lot of healing still to do."

She watched him in silence, soaking in each and every word.

"So I won't kiss you again, though I'd like to."

Why, when she was so afraid of him hurting her, did her heart now drop? Why the sudden sadness?

"I will do all I can to help you, Lillian. To stop those men and to see you are safe and returned to your dress shop."

"Thank you. I don't want to be a burden. I've taken too much of your time already. Though I am thankful for everything you've done for me. I owe you much."

"You are no burden and you owe me nothing."

He turned to look at her again and his eyes searched hers.

She gazed back at him, wishing he would kiss her again, longing for his touch and wondering what she would see in his eyes if he were bathing her again. Wondering what his touch would feel like as he moved the cloth down her body. A deep longing stirred within her.

Frightened by the intensity of the longing she breathed in sharp and her eyes widened.

It was as if her body knew his touch well and longed for it again. The thought frightened her. She didn't remember him bathing her, but it seemed her body did.

There were so many things, which had happened to her, which made her feel a separation between her mind and her body. As if they weren't connected any more.

His eyes stopped searching hers and his expression showed he'd reached a decision.

"I offer you my friendship, if you'll have it, and I swear on my mother's grave that I will not kiss you again unless you want me to. Unless," he paused to emphasize these last words, "you ask me to."

She caught her breath, eyes wide, looking back into his, seeing nothing but sincerity there, somehow knowing he would not break this vow, once he'd given his word.

Holding her breath as time stretched between them, the room seeming to grow smaller, some invisible force pulling both of them together as if in a dream.

"Yes," she said, her breath rushing out. "I would treasure your friendship."

Inside her heart she felt she'd been given a gift. One to treasure. One that was more valuable than a passionate tumble between the two of them might have been.

She would push these bodily cravings she'd developed for him aside.

He treated her with respect. He believed her when she said she didn't know where the gold was and he had been nothing but kind and tender toward her since they had met.

The gift of his friendship was a treasure indeed.

Her heart filled with overwhelming emotion.

A tear slipped out and ran down her face.

"Oh, I don't know why I'm crying."

Silently he watched her, his eyes observant as she smiled and another tear leaked out the other side to run down her cheek.

He gave her a gentle smile. "You've been holding a lot inside."

She smiled back, her gaze now clouded with tears. "Yes."

"I think you should just let it out." He spoke matter-of-factly. As if it were the most natural thing to do. "Let it all go."

This was all it took for her tears to start flowing. It was as if his permission released the flood and she yielded to the sobs that now shook her.

She remembered the pain and the fear. The frustration of wanting to give them what they wanted to make it stop. She remembered how close she came to death. And the brand they'd left her with, the pain of the brand.

It was throbbing even now.

He sat beside her on the bed and held out his arms to hug her.

"Come on."

She moved into his arms and leaned against him as he pulled her close and held her, pulling the blanket around her back. He held her and stroked her hair murmuring words of comfort as he let her cry.

Finally she took one shuddering breath and was still.

He held her, rubbing her back with his warm hands, comforting her until she took a calmer breath.

"It's over now. I've got you. You're safe now."

"Yes," she whispered into his strong chest, feeling his warmth, breathing in his scent.

"It's over." He pulled back, placed one hand on each of her arms and looked into her eyes. "That's the first time you've cried since I cut you down. I'm glad you did, Lillian."

"Yes," she whispered. "I needed that."

"You did." He nodded. "Better now?"

"Yes. Better."

He released her arms and stepped away, turning his back.

"Well I don't know about you, but I've built up a mighty appetite. Dinner is ready. Once you're dressed we can eat."

"All right. I am hungry."

Lillian slipped out of bed and stood. Her body felt lighter than it ever had been and her legs were shaky. She leaned with one hand on the chair in between moving her arms into the shirt and stepping into her skirt. She pulled the chair over to the table to join him and then sat and waited for him to dish out the food.

When he set the plate in front of her, the sight and aroma of the fish made her realize how hungry she was.

They ate in silence and Lillian devoured her food, as she hadn't eaten for days.

Nick watched her, smiling.

"Had enough?"

"Yes," she said, "I couldn't eat another bite."

"Well good, as I'd have to go out and catch more fish. Depending on how they're biting, you might have to wait a while."

"There must be a stream or river nearby."

"Yes ma'am, there is. Would you like me to show you around? The fresh air would do you good."

"That would be nice."

He smiled and held out his arm.

She moved slowly and her body still felt weak, so she accepted the arm he offered her and clung to it until she felt she had her legs back again.

They went outside and he waited while she took care of her personal needs. Then he held out his arm again and she placed her hand upon it. They strolled through the trees. Breathing in deeply she caught the scent of pine and damp leaves.

"It's good to be outside."

"I can imagine after being sick in bed for so many days."

"How many days was I sick? I don't remember much."

"Four days."

"Oh no. I've kept you away from your business deal much too long. I hope this hasn't created a problem for you."

"I hope so too."

They reached the stream, where he'd caught their dinner. He led her to a large black rock beside the stream where they sat together and looked up at the stars.

"It's a beautiful night," he said.

"Yes, very."

They sat in silence gazing at the stars, listening to the night sounds and then he spoke.

"Lillian, now that we have time and you're feeling better, I have some questions. These are hard questions." He watched her face.

She nodded her agreement.

"Why did they brand you? It's a brutal thing to do. Especially to a woman. I've seen and heard a lot." He shook his head. "But never that. I'd like to know why they did that to you."

"I don't know," she shrugged, looking down. "I guess because nothing else had worked and B.T..." she took a deep breath. "He's the meanest man I've ever met."

"Tell me. How did it happen?"

She looked up at him and then her gaze drifted past his shoulder. Then she began.

"B.T.'s men came into the shop one night while I was working and dragged me out and down the street to the saloon. The place was full of angry men who wanted their gold. I tried to tell them I didn't know where it was and my fiancé had stolen from me too, but no one believed me. When B.T. told his men to take me out back and make me talk no one stopped him. The sheriff walked out of the saloon and did nothing. No one did anything to stop B.T." She paused to catch her breath and then said in a low voice, "They didn't even try."

"Who hired the sheriff?"

"B.T."

Nick nodded. "That figures. Then what happened?"

"They tied me up and took me out to the edge of town to a barn. B.T. told me if I didn't tell him where the money was, he was going to mark me. Mark me so I'd be as worthless as the bank notes he held in his hand. He was very angry. He made Grady brand me with an "S" for Shelton Security Bank. He wanted me to see the brand every time I look in the mirror and remember. Grady does all B.T.'s dirty work so B.T. never gets his own hands dirty."

"Who is Grady?"

"B.T.'s hired gun. But that's not all he is. He'll do anything B.T. asks."

She was silent, remembering, frowning. Pain lay beneath her skin where the brand had been drawn and the memory of what Grady had done to her was just as painful in a different way.

"Go on," Nick said.

"Grady kept waving the hot poker in my face and B.T. was yelling. I was so scared I would have told them anything once that poker touched me."

She gasped, her lip starting to tremble and she bit it to hold it still.

"Shh." He touched her lip with his fingertips. "You're safe here with me. You don't have to say more unless you want to." His finger dropped away and her lip quit trembling. "No one is going to hurt you. It's over now."

"When the hot poker touched me, I screamed it burnt so bad. The smell of my own skin burning was...." She closed her eyes again, swallowed and spoke in a whisper. "The stench made me gag. I tried to turn my head away but B.T. held my head and forced me to look at him.

He kept saying if I just told him where the money was he'd make it stop. He'd make the pain go away. I only had to tell him." She shuddered. "But I couldn't."

"It's over now. You will heal. The pain won't last forever."

"I will never forget." Her eyes narrowed. "Grady laughed. I can still hear him laughing."

Nick did not speak but she could feel the anger rolling off of him.

"He would have done more but B.T. stopped him. Said he wanted to leave me alive long enough to think about it long and hard. That made Grady laugh even more and once B.T. left, " She paused and wrapping her arms around herself, looked down, ashamed. "Grady told me he'd give me even more to think long and hard about. Then Grady showed me what he meant by that."

She glanced down, unable to look at him, ashamed of what had been done to her.

"Lillian," Nick cupped her face, making her look at him. "What they did to you was wrong. You have nothing to be ashamed of." His eyes searched hers. "Nothing. None of this was your fault and you did nothing to deserve this."

"I know," she said softly.

He released her chin. "Some men are bad to the core and that's the type you ran into. But you've survived them and that scar will heal." He smiled at her. "You're a strong woman, Lillian Hayes. Stronger than you know." He paused and his eyes searched hers. "Maybe when you look in the mirror the S could stand for survivor and remind you how strong you are."

She gave him a brief smile, but didn't speak. Telling the story had taken what energy she had left right out of her.

"You have a whole lot of living still to do, Lillian."

She nodded, blinking away tears.

He stood and held out his hand to help her up. "What we need now is a good night's sleep. Neither of us have had restful sleep since we met."

She let him help her up and walked beside him back to the cabin.

They didn't speak and it was odd to her how companionable their silence seemed to be. Each time she glanced at his profile, she saw nothing but a calm assured man who was comfortable inside the silence.

Just being in his presence made her felt comfortable and safe.

It seemed incredible that just days ago she'd been afraid of him. No one had ever been as kind to her as Nick had.

She was glad he'd encouraged her to tell her story to him. It felt so much better to have said it and gotten it out of her. It felt good to have one person who believed her, who would not call her a liar. One person who believed what they had done to her was wrong.

When they reached the cabin, he opened the door, looked at her and asked, "Do you know how to shoot?"

"No."

He nodded, waited for her to walk inside then followed her in and said, "Well we will work on that tomorrow morning. I have to leave for a few days to make that business meeting and I want you to know how to defend yourself while I am gone. So get a good night's sleep."

He found a place on the floor, rolled onto his elbow and waited for her to get into bed as if this routine was the most natural thing in the world.

The matter-of-fact way he behaved reassured her more than words would have, so she settled herself in bed as if it was nothing unusual and tried not to be nervous. Perhaps he wasn't attracted to her in the way men usually were, if he'd seen her naked and had made no strong advances toward her now that she was well again. Other than the tenderness of his kiss and the touch of his hands he'd made no move. He would make no aggressive advances toward her and she believed in his promise to her and his gift of friendship.

She was reassured. What then, was this feeling of disappointment that hovered beneath that reassurance?

He waited until she had settled to speak again. "Lillian?"

"Yes?"

"You are a brave woman. I just want you to know that."

"Thank you."

She didn't feel so brave and she lay awake in the darkened room long into the night, wondering why he had to leave her and whether she really could learn how to handle a gun in the morning. She'd always been afraid of guns. No, she wasn't brave at all.

Chapter Seven

Morning came too early.

The birds singing outside were so cheerful. How did they do it every morning?

Lillian almost groaned and rolled over again when she saw Nick was already up and dressed, restlessly moving about the cabin. She could tell by the way he was moving he was anxious to teach her how to shoot so he could ride into town and take care of business.

Well, there is no hope of going to sleep again and it wouldn't be fair to him if she did. He'd put off his meeting long enough for her.

With a sigh, she sat up.

"Feeling all right this morning?"

"Yes, just tired."

She swung her legs out of bed and sat on the edge.

"I wasn't lucky enough to catch any fish this morning, but I boiled some rice."

"That's fine. I'm not all that hungry."

"Nervous?"

"Yes. I've never even held a gun," she said, looking down at her hands with a slight frown.

"I'm going to teach you." His voice was firm. "You'll do fine. This Colt 32 should be easy for you to handle."

So, he was leaving her with Nob Li's gun. Smaller than Nick's gun, it would be better for her, but as far as easy, that she still wasn't sure of.

"I may not be very good at it. I've always been afraid of guns."

"Then it is time to change that. I want to be sure you are able to defend yourself before I ride to town." The confident tone he used told her he believed it to be possible.

Lillian, however wasn't so sure.

She only ate a little bit then after she had cleaned up and washed the dishes she went outside to where he was waiting for her after tending to the horses.

"What am I going to shoot at?"

"I'll show you. Come on."

She followed him back to the stream and when he stopped, she stood next to him, looking around.

"See that log over there?" He pointed to a big old log that lay on its side.

"Yes."

"That's your target."

"Okay."

It was big enough. The question was, could she hit it.

He showed her the gun.

"I've checked it over. It will do you just fine."

She eyed the gun, skeptical. "I've never shot a gun before. Never even held one."

"I know." His voice was patient. "I've already loaded it for you. All you'll have to do is shoot. You'll have five shots."

He held it out for her as she reached for it nervously.

"Put your right finger along the side but do not put it on the trigger till I tell you to."

She immediately felt its weight as she grasped it in her right hand. It was heavier than she thought it would be and her hand shook, though it might have been her nerves. She wondered how she'd hold her hand steady enough to hit anything. She didn't think she could do this.

"Just get the feel of it."

He moved her left hand beneath her right fist, cupping it. "You can use your left hand to steady it if you need to."

She could have, but she was tired of feeling like a helpless female, so she forced herself to only use her right and tried to steady the gun.

"Are you ready?"

"Yes."

Her hand was shaking so he stood behind her and placed his arms around her. He radiated a heat and strength. This was no fever now. She liked the way it felt. Enclosed, safe, warm.

She breathed in as one warm hand closed over each forearm, the heat of his body behind her and his breath in her ear.

"Hold it steady. Now cock the gun. Pull the hammer back." His breath was in her ear, sending tingles through her body. He stood so close she could feel the heat from his body and his nearness was overwhelming. How was she ever going to concentrate?

Following his direction and trying to ignore the way her body was responding to him, she pulled it back with her thumb as far as she could and heard it click.

"Cock it again." His voice rumbled in her ear. "You'll have to do it twice. All the way back." He breathed in her ear again as he spoke and a delightful shiver ran through her.

Concentrate. Pay attention.

She had to ignore the way he was making her feel, so she could learn how to shoot.

It was obvious that here in the west, a woman needed to learn how to protect herself.

"Lillian. You can do this."

She pulled it back further with her thumb until it stopped.

"That's it." His voice held approval and encouragement. "Now take aim." He moved her arms where he thought they should be. "Line it up like this with the sight. Before you aim, take a breath, hold it then let it out slow when you pull the trigger." He stepped back away from her as if he knew what a distraction he was.

She breathed in concentrating.

"Now squeeze the trigger when you're ready."

She squeezed.

Bang!

"Oh my!"

The gun had pulled up as she shrieked and the shot had gone high over the log.

Smoke billowed around the gun and she squinted waiting for the smoke to clear.

"I missed."

"It's all right. You're just getting used to the feel of the gun."

"It's heavy. Why does it jump like that?"

"It wasn't the gun that jumped, it was you."

She wasn't sure she'd ever get used to the feel of the gun, but she could get used to the feel of Nick's arms around her. She very much liked the way that felt.

"Try again. This time don't jerk the trigger. Squeeze it slow." He guided her back into position again and this time he silently waited for her to cock the gun and take aim.

"That's it. Now squeeze."

She squeezed slowly.

Click. Click. Bang!

"Oh!"

The gun pulled up again, less than the first time and she hadn't shrieked, though it still startled her.

How did one ever get used to this?

She was still nervous and her shot had missed.

She coughed from the smoke, which had blown into her face.

"I can't do this."

"The hell you can't. Shoot again."

She was ready to give up. He didn't understand. She couldn't do this. She was jumpy and not hitting a thing.

He moved to take the gun from her, looked at it then placed it back in her hand. "This time you're going to hit it." He stepped back. "Try again."

She listened but she didn't believe him as self-doubt filled her mind.

"Lillian you have three more shots. And we will keep at this until you hit that log."

"I just don't think I can." Her hand was still shaky, the gun was heavy and her thumb was already tired from fighting to pull the hammer back.

She looked at her slim fingers, more used to soft fabrics and thin needles, not farm implements and tools.

His voice interrupted her thoughts. "Think about what those men did to you. What are you going to do when you see them again? What if that log was Grady?"

She squinted at the log and the squint turned into a glare.

If that log was Grady...

She cocked the gun back by herself. Click. Click. She aimed without hesitation and pulled the trigger.

Bang!

This time she made no sound at all, only watched the smoke rise and listened as the log took the shot, sending up splinters

"I hit the log!"

"Yes, ma'am, that you did."

A great satisfaction filled her. The shot wasn't perfect, the gun had still pulled and she had trouble holding it but she'd hit that log. If it had been a man she would have hit him too.

"Not bad for a lady from back east who never learned to ride or shoot. Not bad."

She turned to him and gave him a great big smile. "I've been told I'm a fast learner."

"Yes, you are."

He smiled and his eyes settled on her in a way that made her feel all unsettled inside.

"Here, I'll reload it for you."

She handed him the gun and he opened it, moved the revolving cylinder and poured powder into the cylinder chambers then capped the nipples.

"Remember the barrel will get hotter each time you shoot it." He loaded the gun as if he'd done it a thousand times and it was second nature. "And keep it dry so your powder stays dry."

"I'll remember." She placed a hand on his forearm and he paused, looking into her eyes. "Thank you for teaching me," she said.

"Lillian," his voice warmed, "there are plenty of things I'd like to teach you if you'd ask me and if I had more time," he winked, "but I have to go meet with a man about those horses."

Much as he'd enjoyed teaching her to shoot, wrapping his arms around her, much as he wanted to take her into that house right now and teach her other things, he needed to go.

It was just as well they be apart for a day or two. His dreams had been full of her last night and they'd had to stand close for her shooting lesson. He kept having the urge to kiss her. She was rapidly becoming a distraction. One he couldn't afford right now.

He had horses to sell and he was already five days late meeting the buyer. If the deal hadn't gone sour, it wouldn't take him long to set up the sale to Mr. Kingston and get back to her. Then he'd deliver the horses and take care of the men who had hurt her.

He handed her the gun. "Keep it near and if in doubt shoot first, ask questions later."

"Yes, I will." She watched him saddle his horse.

He'd gathered his things while she was still sleeping.

"I have to leave now. But you're going to be fine."

She nodded, "I'll shoot if I have to. Don't worry. How many horses do you have?"

"Twenty in the canyon, not counting these two. More back at the ranch. If this deal goes well, I'll be bringing more horses later."

"Are they all those spotted horses?"

"They're called appaloosas."

"Well, they're real pretty."

"Yes, they are. I'm partial to them. Best horses I've ever had."

Much as he enjoyed talking with her, watching the expressions cross her face, he needed to get on the road. All this chatter was only delaying him. He was already late. He'd made sure there was enough wood for the fire, he'd caught several fish for her to cook before she'd even woke up and he'd taught her to shoot this afternoon. Taking care of Lillian had put him way behind schedule. The sooner he took care of business, the sooner he could return to her.

"I'll be back in two days. You'll be safe here. Stay out of sight if anyone comes around and keep that gun handy."

"I will."

"Good." He went to saddle up his horse.

She stood watching him in silence.

Nick wondered what she was thinking. She seemed lost in thought. He hoped she wasn't worried about staying out here by herself.

He mounted his horse, gave her a smile and said, "I'll be back as soon as I can."

She nodded. "Hurry back."

He waved and rode away, thinking of how Lillian looked standing quietly watching him go. She was beautiful with the light catching her hair and a wistful expression on her face, unspoken words in her eyes. Eyes, which promised much under better and different circumstances.

Shelton was a fool to have abandoned her and more than a fool to leave Lillian to face his crimes.

He urged his horse on, anxious to get to town and take care of business. He wouldn't leave her alone any longer than was necessary. Though he would make sure he picked up a pretty dress for her before he returned. She'd not mentioned it again since her fever broke, but he knew it was a longing she had. A pretty dress might help her to feel less broken.

He wished she could see what he saw in her and wished she would realize how strong and how beautiful she was.

Lillian was safe enough at the cabin, but if anyone did come by who had bad intentions, he hoped she'd have steady enough nerves to shoot the gun he'd left with her and that she'd remember what he told her. "Take a breath, aim, and shoot first. Ask questions later."

*****

Lillian watched him go and wished she could be riding to town with him. But he was right. It wasn't safe for her to go back yet. She waited till he'd gone then went down to the creek where she stripped off her clothes to bathe and then scrubbed them and laid them out to dry while she stepped into the water to bathe herself.

There was no one about and she took advantage of the fact she was alone. She stepped into the cool stream and waded into the middle until the water came up to her waist. The current moved past and between her legs, the feeling one she had never experienced before, being a city girl from back east.

Taking handfuls of the clear water she scooped the water up and over her head, running it through her hair, closing her eyes and taking deep cleansing breaths. With each breath and each scoop poured upon her, she imagined the water washing her clean throughout her body, as the current carried everything dirty and ugly away. Over and over the water poured down her body until at last she felt clean and whole again.

When she was done, she stood, water streaming down her body, letting the sun and air begin to dry her skin as the birds sang.

She looked down at the mark in her breast.

The "S" was not the angry red color of the fresh brand or of the infection but had even started to heal. It now itched slightly. Nick was right. It would heal soon but how she viewed this mark, which would be with her for the rest of her life, was important.

Survivor. Yes, that's what I am.

If anyone were ever to ask her what it meant, all she would say is, it means I survive.

To survive was a different kind of strength. A strength that settled deep within the bones in a way no mark made on the flesh could.

She sat on the black rock and waited, closing her eyes and listening to the birds and to the beating of her heart while inside of her a great healing began. By the time she was dry and ready to reach for her clothing, which had dried, she felt a peacefulness settling within her.

Pulling Nick's shirt around her, her thoughts turned to Nick. She wished she could have told him exactly how she felt now and she wished she could thank him for what he had done for her.

He had done so much and yet he had asked for nothing.

Nick was quite a man. She missed him already and looked forward to his return.

*****

Reaching Garwood, Nick headed directly for the Bon Ton Saloon.

It looked to be a successful establishment. Polished mahogany wood and a gleaming brass foot rail at the bar, the usual things you would find in a saloon. A red faro table, which looked brand new.

Over the bar hung an enormous painting of a nude raven haired woman lounging on a couch, her long wavy tresses barely covering the tips of her breasts, her leg bent to shield her mound. It would have been an expensive painting and one you wouldn't see outside of one of the finer establishments with women for hire. Every decoration in the place spoke of money and success.

Three women moved about the saloon. A redhead, a brunette, and a blonde.

The blonde appeared to be the saloon girl. Her job would be to encourage the men to drink. To dance a little, sing a little. The brunette looked too young to be in the place, so he couldn't quite place her. The red-haired woman was the kind you might take upstairs if you had coin enough.

Now on the surface, such a fancy bar might not be unexpected or seem out of place. In some towns, where gambling and saloons lined the streets and miners emptied their pockets, this saloon might not have stood out so much.

Garwood was not such an established town. The mines never yielded enough gold for the town to be as prosperous as some of the other boomtowns, though the miners had some success. Just enough to keep them going in hopes of a big strike. The Bon Ton Saloon was obviously the richest building.

Nick went over and leaned one elbow on the bar.

"Whiskey."

The young bartender set a glass in front of him along with a bottle. He seemed unsure of himself and Nick wondered why the owner of the Bon Ton Saloon would hire a lad so green around the ears to serve his customers their drinks.

"I'm looking for Mr. Kingston."

The boy gave him a strange look "Why?"

"My business is with him. Is the saloon owner in?"

The bartender nodded yes and laid down his towel before heading to a back room.

Nick sipped his whiskey and waited.

The bartender returned trailing a tall man with wavy brown hair slicked back and a thin mustache. The man was dressed in a black suit with a white shirt, a red and black silk vest and shiny black boots.

Nick took an immediate dislike to the man, though he had no reason to. Other than he had the kind of eyes Nick did not trust.

"I'm Mr. Kingston. You asked for me?"

"Nicholas Brace." Nick extended his hand.

The man's entire demeanor changed and he shook Nick's hand. "Glad you made it. Let's retire to my office."

Nick nodded and turned to pick up his glass, to finish it off quick, but Kingston said, "Leave it. I'll share my private stock with you."

They walked toward the back office, Kingston leading the way.

"You have trouble on the trail? You're five days late."

"Bad weather up north slowed me down. Had to make a detour."

"Must have been quite a detour. I trust the stock is well."

"Yes, they are."

"Excellent." Kingston opened the door and gestured to Nick to enter. "I'm looking forward to seeing these appaloosas everyone is talking about."

Nick stepped in and Kingston moved behind his desk. "Have a seat. Make yourself comfortable."

As Nick sat, Kingston pulled out two glasses and a bottle.

"Now this is the good stuff."

He poured them each a glass and raised it to Nick. "To successful new enterprises."

Nick forced a smile and toasted back. "To success."

They each swallowed then Kingston set his glass down and leaned forward with his elbows on his desk; his hands poised together and a gleam in his eye. "You'll want to see the money."

"Yes." Nick nodded.

"There will be plenty more once my contact with the government comes through with a contract for more horses." He chuckled. "This will be profitable for both of us."

"I can supply as many as you need. Just let me know."

Kingston opened up a satchel, which was atop his desk, took out a wad of bank notes and set them on the desk, counting them.

Nick looked down at them, reading the bank notes upside down.

Shelton Security Bank. *He's trying to pass worthless paper script on to me, thinking I won't know they aren't worth the paper they're printed on.*

He kept his face neutral and looked back at Kingston. "I don't want paper. That wasn't our deal. You promised gold."

A quick flash in Kingston's eye betrayed his surprise before his lids hooded again.

"Yes, yes I did." Kingston smiled. "And you promised to be here five days ago. Of course the bank is closed now and won't be open until tomorrow."

"I'd still prefer the gold, like we'd agreed upon."

"I'm a busy man. Yet you want me to take time out of my day to exchange these at the bank for gold, to purchase horses I've yet to see. Horses that should have been here by now." Kingston put the money back into the bag and closed it. He pushed his chair back to stand. "Why don't we go look at them now. See if they're all you say they are."

"I don't have them all with me."

Kingston frowned.

"Only the one I rode in on, which I would be glad to show you."

Kingston stared, clearly unhappy.

"When will I be seeing the others?"

"In two days, when you have the gold."

"Mr. Brace." His mouth spread into a thin-lipped smile and he leaned his palms against the desktop. "You are a cautious man. You clearly don't trust me. And your delays do not speak well of your business dealings. But we have a deal. I want those horses. We can work this out. Relax. You stay here at the saloon as my guest tonight. No bad feelings. Your food and drinks are on me and if you require female companionship that is also available to you."

Nick stood. "No, I'd best get back to the horses. I will have them here the day after tomorrow, toward evening, which will give you plenty of time to visit the bank."

Kingston straightened "I think you will find the gold much heavier than bank notes would be. It would be much easier to travel with these bank notes. Much safer."

"Nevertheless, I prefer gold."

"You are a stubborn man."

Nick nodded. "Many would agree."

"Well, as I cannot change your mind," Kingston smiled thinly, the smile not quite reaching his cold eyes. "I will see you in two days, with the rest of the horses."

Nick nodded, even more sure he disliked Kingston. "Good."

If the man would provide the gold, he could buy the horses. Kingston had no way of knowing Nick knew the paper script was worthless, which meant the man would cheat him if he could. It wasn't the first time Nick had run into a cheat when horse-trading, but he'd never been cheated yet. If Kingston had gold, Nick would still go through with the deal.

He was a man who kept his word.

Though he doubted Kingston's ability to procure that much gold if he did not already hold it in reserve. And if Lillian's fiancé had taken off with all the man's gold those bank notes were likely the only currency he had.

"Well then. I will walk you out and take a look at that horse before you go."

Nick nodded. "I think you'll be pleased."

The men went outside and Kingston examined the horse. Then he nodded. "This mare is a fine piece of horse flesh. I look forward to seeing the others."

One of Kingston's men came to the door of the saloon and shouted out, "B.T."

Kingston turned his head and Nick froze.

Kingston and B.T. were the same man. He didn't know why he hadn't made the connection before. The pieces now fell into place and Nick had to control his anger before Kingston noticed. He schooled his features and grasped the reins of his horse.

"There's a package for you just arrived."

"I'll be in shortly." Kingston turned back to Nick. "See you in two days."

Nick gave a curt nod and watched Kingston's back as he went into the building.

Chapter Eight

Nick visited the mercantile store for supplies before riding back to the cabin. All the way back to the cabin he kept rethinking the deal. This was business and they'd made a deal. He was a man of his word and he would keep it.

But he didn't like it. The whole deal now stunk, like something gone rancid.

He'd keep his word. What he did after, that was another thing altogether.

For now, he needed to get back to check on Lillian and the horses.

*****

B.T. walked into his office where several of his men were standing around the package, which turned out to be Nob Li's body.

"Get that trash off my good carpet." B.T. scowled. "I didn't tell you to bring him here. Take him to the undertakers. Have you found the woman yet?"

"No sign of her."

"She's still alive. I don't trust that horse trader. Grady, you follow him."

"Yes, sir." Grady left to see where the horse trader had headed.

It wasn't long until he returned.

B.T. frowned at him. "I told you to follow the horse trader."

"I did. Thought you would want to know he just bought a dress in the mercantile."

B.T.'s eyes narrowed. "A dress."

"Yes, sir."

"That's a strange thing for a man traveling alone to buy."

Grady nodded.

"Follow him when he leaves town and find out where he's keeping those horses. Keep an eye out for the woman and," he smiled. "Take Carl with you. Keep an eye on him. He may let something slip if he's away from here."

"Yes, sir."

B.T. smiled. "If he tries to ride off, let him go and follow him. So you give him every chance to do that once you know where the horses are. He could lead you straight to the woman."

Grady started out the door.

"And Grady? Keep it clean this time. As if you weren't there."

*****

Lillian saw a rider coming and hurried back inside the cabin, gun ready.

But as the rider came closer, she saw it was only Nick. She laid the gun down and a sense of relief came over her. She sat down on a chair to wait for him, suddenly feeling shy and nervous.

How would things be between them when they were together again? What had he found out in town?

Nick settled the horse then entered the cabin, carrying a brown package under his arm. "Brought you something." He held it out to her. "Thought you might like it."

Surprise spread across her face.

"A gift? For me?"

She reached out for it and he handed it to her.

"Yes." He smiled. "I hope you like it."

She placed it on her lap and hurrying to open the brown paper, like a child opening a birthday gift, she tore the package open.

"A dress?" She stood and held it up as it unfolded. "Oh my," she breathed.

The soft and feminine white dress had small purple violets embroidered on it. She'd seen this dress in the mercantile and thought it was the prettiest one she'd seen from back east. So delicate and pretty.

"It's beautiful." She turned shining eyes up at Nick who stood watching her.

"I'm glad you like it."

"But it's too dear. You shouldn't have spent so much."

He shrugged. "I wanted to." His gaze upon her was soft. "You deserve something pretty to wear."

Her hand caressed the embroidered purple flowers. "I've always loved violets. When I was a little girl I used to pick them for my grandmother and she would place them in a teacup and set it upon her writing desk. My grandfather was a minister and she wrote many letters to her sisters back home."

"Where was home?"

"Ireland. She came over with her mother when she was a baby."

"That must be where you got your red hair. From your grandmother."

"Yes." She smiled. "Grandmother had hair just like mine. I've always been told I resemble her."

"Then your grandmother must have been a beautiful woman."

Lillian blushed. "Thank you. Yes. She was."

"Are you feeling all right now?"

She clasped the dress to her chest, feeling as if he'd given her back a piece of herself. The violet dress would remind her of happy memories of her grandmother. The dress had already made her happier than she'd thought she'd ever be again.

"Yes, much better now. Thank you." She beamed up at him.

A deep smile filled his face as if he'd caught some of her happiness.

She was stuck by how tall and handsome he was. He had the most handsome smile she had ever seen.

"Good." The smile never left his eyes as they searched hers.

She lost all sense of time when he looked at her like that.

He cleared his throat as if he needed to clear his head as well and then turned to go out the door. "I brought a few other things. If you'll cook dinner, I'll go check on the horses."

"I'd be happy to. Thank you again for the dress."

"My pleasure, Lillian."

He went out to get another package, brought it back in and handed it to her.

Setting it on the table, she opened it and looked up at him. "Beans again? Is that all you eat?"

"Well, I've been a little too busy to go fishing."

"Okay. Beans it is."

"Thank you, darlin'." He winked and went out the door, calling back, "I'll be back soon."

*****

Behind the trees Grady and Carl sat watching Nick come out of the cabin.

"Are we going to follow him?" Carl said.

"Not yet. There's someone in that cabin with him. Doesn't sound like he's going far. We'll wait to see if they come out," Grady said.

Time went on and soon they could smell the beans cooking. Carl's stomach growled.

"That smells good," Carl said.

Grady grunted acknowledgement of that fact but gave no other response.

"I'm hungry."

"Like I ain't?"

"We could ride back to town. Get a good meal. No one is going to come out of there tonight. We could sleep in a good bed, ride back out here in the morning."

"Shut it. We ain't going anywhere."

"But we didn't bring food, or blankets." Carl's voice turned whiney.

Grady pulled his knife out as Carl's voice trailed away.

"Told you to shut it."

Carl backed away from the blade and didn't say another word.

*****

Lillian slipped on the dress and wished she had a mirror so she could see herself. It felt so good to be wearing a dress so new and light and pretty. So feminine it made her feel pretty again. The violets reminded her of her grandmother and took her back to a time when she'd been young and innocent and believed all men were good like her grandfather. Before she'd grown up, moved west and been shown otherwise.

She glanced down at her breast.

No one could see the brand now. Not even a hint of it. No one would ever know unless she told them or someone else did.

She placed her hand over the wound, which had been covered with a bandage.

At least it won't bleed through the white. No one will know.

Part of her wished she did not have to go back to the town, even for her things. Yet there were things there she needed to have.

I'll sell my shop and move far away where no one will ever know I've been branded. Where no one has ever heard of this town or my fiancé and no one knows what happened here.

The dress was a bit snug. She pulled at it here and there, thinking about seams and how she'd need to let it out in a few places.

If she'd sewn the dress.

Then she caught herself. Sometimes it was hard appreciating store bought things when you could sew for yourself. The embroidery and fabric really were lovely. Finding fault with things was a new habit she'd acquired from spending time with her cousin and it was time for that to stop right now.

She smoothed her hands down her hips across the fabric, thinking of how Nick had bought the dress for her and what a kind thing that was to do when he could have just gone to her dress shop.

Now why hadn't he done that?

She'd ask him when he returned.

*****

Nick opened the cabin door and took in the sight of Lillian in her new dress looking very much like the lady she was as she stood stirring their dinner which smelled mighty good.

Now this was a sight to come home to. Something he'd never had. For the first time in his life he understood why a man might desire this. He shut the door behind him and leaned his shotgun against the wall.

"Sure does smell good."

"Hungry?" Lillian ladled out the beans into his bowl.

"Yes, ma'am."

She put an extra scoop in. "Here you go then."

"Thank you." He carried it over to the table and sat, waiting for her to join him.

Just before she turned toward him to come sit down, he saw her bare feet poking out beneath the new dress, which fit her so well. Lillian had an hourglass figure and the dress displayed it to her best advantage.

"Thank you for the dress," she said with a smile. "I will pay you back once I have my money."

"No need to. It was my pleasure. And Lillian?" His eyes darkened.

"Yes?"

"You look beautiful."

"Thank you." She blushed becomingly.

"I mean that."

"I know you do."

"I'm sorry I didn't bring you shoes. If you tell me what size you need I will bring a pair back when I come back from selling the horses."

"Thank you. I do have a pair of shoes back at my dress shop. Why didn't you go there?"

"They may be watching your dress shop to see if you return. This was safer for you."

"Well thank you. Did your deal go well?"

"The deal is still on. I'll stay here one night then head back to town with the horses in the morning."

"Good. Did you have a chance to ask about my store? To look around?"

"No, not on this trip. But I will next time."

Lillian sat quietly eating. It was the longest he'd ever known a woman to keep quiet during a meal. Most of the women he'd known felt the need to fill any silences in a conversation. He wasn't sure how to read her. Was she upset he hadn't checked on her store? She hadn't seemed so and had accepted his explanation.

The way she sat watching Nick told him she had something on her mind. He decided to watch her back, while enjoying his meal. She certainly was good to look at. A feast for his eyes. He smiled to himself and took another bite.

Finally she spoke.

"How were the horses?"

"Just fine. Haven't lost a one," he said.

"Good."

He took in a deep breath and then let loose a sigh.

He noted the snug way the dress fit her. He tried not to let his eyes linger on her breasts though the way the dress fit made it hard not to, especially when she took a deep breath like that.

She toyed with her food and he watched the way she moved the spoon around her plate. Whatever was bothering her, she was having trouble bringing it up. She'd gone from watching him to watching her plate.

"Something troubling you, Lillian?"

Her gaze darted up and him and her words came out all in a rush.

"I want to go with you tomorrow," she said. "I want to check on my shop and also see justice done."

"We can do that next time, after I deliver the horses."

"I'll help you with them."

"Lillian," he shook his head. "You don't know the first thing about herding horses. And I don't need help."

"Please, Nick."

She can look at me with those pleading green eyes all she likes, but she isn't going tomorrow.

"No, you're not going with me."

She opened her mouth to argue but he cut her off.

"I've told you I'll take you next time and I'm not going to argue with you about it. You're staying here where you're safe until I get back."

Even if he'd wanted to take her with him, he wasn't about to put her within arm's reach of B.T. This wasn't the time to tell her B.T. and the man he was dealing with tomorrow were one and the same. No, he'd tell her when he got back. He'd tell her after he took care of things. The last place she should be is around any of the men who had hurt her.

No, she was safe here and here she was going to stay. He had enough to deal with without worrying about her all the way there and then having to keep her safe in that town where everyone was against her. He didn't think much of the town or of the people in it.

She'd stopped talking and her mouth was now formed into a pout. A most kissable pout he did his best to ignore.

They finished their meal in silence.

Well fine, if that's the way she wants it. She can pout all night if she wants to. It isn't going to change a thing.

Had circumstances been different he would have spent time kissing away that pout.

He went outside, checked on the horses and tired to put thoughts of kissing her out of his mind. In a way it was good he was leaving tomorrow. Lillian distracted him too much for her own good or for his. She'd been on his mind constantly from the moment he'd first seen her.

The long ride to town would help him clear his head. It was essential to doing what needed to be done.

He turned in early, planning to rise at dawn.

*****

They said their good nights and Lillian lay awake in the dark cabin wondering how she could convince him to let her go to town with him tomorrow.

Finally when he cleared his throat and coughed, she realized he was still awake.

"Nick?"

"Yes."

"I need to ride to town with you tomorrow morning. I've got to check on my store. Every day it looks abandoned is a day more things can be stolen."

"Darlin,' we've been around this before. You know going into town isn't safe."

"But I need to."

"No." He cut her off. "You don't need to. I have enough to take care of with wrangling the horses without you along to look after. Go to sleep."

She didn't respond, though he'd hurt her feelings.

He was right.

He'd done nothing but take care of her since he'd found her.

But she had learned to shoot and she could learn to ride a horse too. Even if she had to teach herself. Tomorrow, once he'd left, she would get up on that horse.

She'd teach herself and then she'd follow him because she wasn't staying here. Not for one day more.

With that thought she curled up and went to sleep.

*****

Nick lay awake in the dark wondering at Lillian's silence and whether he'd hurt her feelings. She'd spoken with such emotion and then gone completely silent when he cut her off.

But he'd spoken the truth. He'd move faster, get his business taken care of then see to her business. He'd see that she was on her feet again, shoes and all, soon. She needed to trust him.

"Lillian?" He'd say as much, reassure her and apologize for cutting her short.

She didn't answer. Listening closer he heard the sound of a very soft snore.

He threw one arm over his head.

Women. Who could figure them?

It was way beyond him. He had a long ride tomorrow and needed to get to sleep himself.

In the morning Nick skipped breakfast, drank down a cup of coffee and waited for Lillian to speak more than two words to him.

So far, "good morning," "thank you," and "no" had been the extent of her half of the conversation.

She was obviously still upset with him and he'd had enough.

"Listen, I apologize for cutting you off last night, but I was tired."

"I would like to go with you today."

"No. You're not going."

He watched her purse her lips.

Those kissable, rosy lips. He had to stop thinking about kissing her right now.

"I'll hurry back, I promise. Then I'll help you."

"Fine."

The woman was exasperating.

If it weren't for his promise not to kiss her until she asked him, he'd kiss her right now. She was going to drive him crazy with all that pouting soon and she looked so fetching in that dress.

He needed to focus. He didn't dare take her with him to meet with B.T.

Of course she didn't know he was meeting with B.T. He'd spared her that detail. She had enough on her mind.

He loaded the gun and handed it to her.

"Remember, stay close to the cabin and keep that gun handy. If in doubt, shoot first and ask questions later."

He didn't like to think of what might happen to her if anyone got close enough to take the gun away from her.

She only nodded and stood watching him with a strange look in her eyes before saying, "Hurry back."

He wondered what she was thinking.

"I will darlin', don't worry. Just a couple days then I'll be back."

*****

Dawn didn't come early enough for Grady, who came near to shooting Carl more than once, just to shut him up.

When the horse trader came out of the cabin and mounted his horse, Grady said, "I'm going to follow him. You stay here. Watch whoever's in that cabin. Don't do anything stupid. Wait for me to circle back."

The look he gave Carl said he fully expected Carl to do just that.

"I don't see why I have to stay here."

Grady touched his knife and Carl shut up.

*****

Carl waited till both men had ridden away and then moved closer to the cabin.

"Nick?"

The woman's voice was soft enough he almost didn't hear her.

He waited for a minute, but whoever she was, she wasn't coming out. So he moved closer, feeling cockier.

She was just a woman, alone. No reason not to look in and see who she was.

Carl peered through the window and his jaw dropped before closing into a grin.

Cousin Lil all dolled up.

His day had just improved. Maybe his cousin wasn't so dumb after all. His luck had changed.

She had to have that gold. She had herself a new man and a fancy new dress bought with it. Moving to the door, he kicked it open and she shrieked.

"Hello, cousin. Got you a pretty new dress? Store-bought, too." He sneered. "No more late nights sewing other ladies' dresses, now you've got all that gold."

Chapter Nine

Lillian shrieked.

Her gaze flickered to where Nick had left the gun and then back to her cousin.

"Surprised to see me, Lil?" He laughed.

"Yes. Very." She frowned at him. "Get out."

"Now that's no way to talk to your cousin, your kin." He leaned an arm on the doorframe, looming over her. "I know your mama taught you better than that. Just like she taught you how to cook. I'm mighty hungry. You should be offering me breakfast and coffee. Where are your manners?"

She stood glaring at him before beginning to back toward the gun.

"I lost them shortly before being strung up over a mine shaft."

"Now surely you can't blame that one on me."

Watch me.

"After everything I've done for you, helping you set up your dress shop, introducing you to everyone in town, even that rich fiancé you let get away. Course you don't need him. With enough gold, we don't need anybody. You and me, Lil, we can go west to the coast and set up house there rich as kings and nobody knowing where the money came from. With your fine east coast manners, you could pull that off."

He talks and talks and not one word of it is the truth.

How did she never see it before?

The more he talked, the more she saw through him now.

She wasn't buying any of what he was saying. Then as he saw she hadn't softened her attitude toward him one bit, his mood changed, crossing his face like a violent summer storm.

"Stupid bitch." He reached out to grab her.

Lillian lunged for the gun and he missed her.

She grabbed the gun, turning toward him as she pulled the hammer back.

Click.

"You're no kin of mine."

"Give me the damn gun, Lillian."

Click.

"Or you'll what?" He reached out to grab the gun.

She squeezed.

Boom!

*****

Nick pulled his horse to a stop when he heard the shot.
Lillian.
He had to get back.
Turning his horse, he urged his mount into a gallop, praying she was all right.
It was a damn good thing he hadn't ridden too far to have heard the shot. Another hour and he would have been.
Racing to the cabin he listened for another shot and prayed he'd reach her in time.

*****

Grady cursed and moved to be out of Nick's line of sight once again.
Damn Carl. If he messed this up for me.
B.T. did not tolerate failures and Grady had never failed him. Carl on the other hand...
Grady couldn't wait until B.T. gave him the okay to take care of Carl.
He hoped whoever was in that cabin hadn't taken away that pleasure for him.
They were supposed to return to B.T. as if they'd never been there, leaving no trace. Now there might be a body to deal with.
Clean up was the least favorite part of his job.
Either way, Carl had made a mess for him. Grady would bet money on that.

*****

Lillian stood back against the wall holding the smoking gun, arms shaking. She coughed once from the smoke and her eyes teared up.
"Lillian?" Carl leaned his head to the side looking at her in amazement through the smoke as his hand went to his belly "You shot me? You don't know how to shoot."
"I do now."
Her hands shook terribly but her voice was firm.
"Your own kin. How could you?"
"You're no kin of mine. Not any more."
She pulled the hammer back again.
Click.
"If you come any closer I will shoot you again."
Click.
He froze then leaned onto the chair. "I got to sit, Lil."
"You go ahead and sit. But you stay in that chair and keep your hands still."
"Lillian, you going to let me sit here and bleed to death? Do nothing to

help me? After all I've done for you?"

"You never did anything for me that wasn't to benefit you. I don't owe you a thing. I'm done listening to you."

"Lil," he spoke once more before blood rushed out of his mouth and his eyes glazed.

She would never know what he'd wanted to say.

*****

When Nick reined up beside the cabin, gun pulled and ready, all was quiet.

With a worried frown he eased open the door.

The first thing he saw was Lillian leaning in a squat against the far wall, arms shaking, her gun pointed at a man in a chair. A man who wasn't moving and from the way his head was slumped over was likely dead.

"Lil? You okay? Are you hurt?"

"I shot my cousin," Lillian whispered. "I killed Carl."

Nick could see the anguish in her eyes.

She stared down at the gun in her shaking hands.

He walked over to her and knelt, easing the gun from her hands. He uncocked the gun and laid it aside.

Peering into her eyes he said, "You okay, Angel?"

She started to shake, tears filling her eyes.

"Come here, Angel."

He helped her to stand and pulled her into his arms, holding her close.

She sank into his warm embrace.

His hand rubbed up and down her back, his strength and warmth comforting her and she exhaled, tension beginning to fade away.

"He was my cousin," she whispered. "The only family I had left. But he was no good. He didn't care about me, only the gold."

"Gold has turned many a man's head. Lillian, you did what you had to do."

"I remembered how he was as a little boy back when he visited. Mama was always so good to him." When she took a breath in, her body shook.

"It's over now," he said. "Let it go."

She cried for her cousin, for what her last remaining family should have been but wasn't and for herself, for how she'd been treated and how she was now alone in the world.

Nick held her until she was through crying, and then pulled back.

Looking into each other's eyes just inches apart their gazes searched each other's then rested, neither looking away nor seeing anything else.

She longed for him to kiss her. It was a longing stronger than anything she'd ever known. Though she'd told herself after Mr. Shelton ran off that she was done with men, ever since Nick had rescued her, her thoughts turned more and more to how Nick's lips would feel upon hers, to how it would feel to be in his arms.

She realized her gaze had lingered on his lips again and looked back up into his eyes.

Then he smiled, his gaze dropping to her lips then up again. "You have to ask, Angel. Remember?"

His smiled deepened as if he wanted to kiss her.

Her breath caught and she breathed out a, "yes."

"Yes?" He teased. "Yes what?"

"Yes, kiss me, Nick. Please."

His lips lowered onto hers in a soft, gentle kiss as if he tasted her for the first time, savoring the moment. A kiss so tender, slow and deliberate it was completely unlike the rushed kisses she'd experienced before. A kiss that gave more than it took.

Lillian responded as her lips parted, letting him in, tasting him as well.

She could have stayed here just like this, kissing him all day, but he pulled back then cupped her jaws tenderly in both hands.

"Darlin', I wish we could spend more time here like this, but I have to get those horses to town."

"I don't want to stay behind. Please let me come with you."

He ran a thumb across her bottom lip, causing it to tingle.

"I want you to be safe."

She watched him in silence, as he seemed to be considering it, her eyes pleading when her words wouldn't.

Words hadn't swayed him before despite her reasoning, nor had her silence, but maybe if she pleaded with him, explaining how she felt…

"Please Nick. I don't feel safe here by myself now. I'm too frightened to stay here alone."

His gaze switched to one of concern as he considered what she'd said and his tone grew even more serious. "How do you think your cousin found you?"

"I don't know."

"Well, this has changed things. If he could find you, so could the others. We don't know if he told them where he thought you were or where he was going. So you can't stay here alone now. It looks like you're coming with me."

She clasped her hands together. "Oh, thank you. I promise not to be a burden. You won't have to worry about me."

His jaw clenched and he reached for her, pulling her in close to hold her in his arms. She wrapped her arms around him and he kissed the top of her head.

"Angel, I can't help but worry about you. But I'd worry more if you weren't nearby where I knew you were safe."

"I feel safe when I'm with you."

His arms tightened around her. He'd hoped she would feel safe with him. Hoped what had happened to her hadn't made her afraid of all men forever.

"I'm glad to hear that, Angel. Real glad."

She gazed up at him. "No man has ever made me feel safe the way that you do."

He held her for another moment looking down into her eyes as his smile deepened and his heart swelled. He wanted to kiss her right now, wanted to sweep her away onto a soft bed where he would kiss every inch of her body, showing her the love and tenderness she deserved. But she might not be ready for that yet.

He'd bide time and hope some day she would be. They didn't have time for that now anyway. Not until he'd taken care of things and made sure she was safe from the men who hard hurt her. He wanted that more than anything.

Getting control of his emotions he pulled back holding her arms and looking into her eyes. "You'll have to promise to do as I say without question or hesitation when I tell you to."

He'd be riding her straight into B.T.'s clutches if he weren't careful. If she wasn't careful. And he couldn't even tell her.

"Yes, Nick, I promise I will. Thank you."

"No need to thank me. We need to get going though. There's a body to bury."

*****

Grady, watching the cabin from up on a hill did a double take when he saw the woman come out of the cabin.

Lillian Hayes. What a surprise.

Grady smirked as he contemplated for a moment whether to shoot the man and take the woman and the horses, but decided against it. One without the other he might have. But it would be a whole lot easier to let the horse trader handle both the horses and the woman.

Let him do all the work. There was plenty of time to wait for the right moment.

B.T. would be more than pleased. The horses, the woman, and the gold. B.T. might even give Grady another bonus. He could even give Grady the woman. One sample of her hadn't been enough. He'd ask B.T. for time off and then he'd bring the woman back to this cabin.

She could beg and scream all she wanted here. It was a perfect little love nest.

Chuckling, Grady thought of all the things he would do to her.

When the horse trader came out carrying Carl's body, Grady spat on the ground in disgust.

Damn fool got himself killed by a woman. B.T. wouldn't like it. But he'd soon forget. Once Grady delivered horses, the woman and the gold, Carl wouldn't matter.

He waited till they'd buried the body. When they headed back to round up the horses, he rode back to town to tell B.T.

The herd would slow them down.

Grady rode hard, the sooner to give B.T. the news and to prepare.

Chapter Ten

Grady rode up to the saloon dismounted and tied his horse to the rail. He went up the steps and through the swinging doors of the quiet saloon. "Where's B.T.?"

"He's back in his office," the barkeep polished a glass.

"What's going on?" B.T. said as he came to stand in the back of the room just outside his office after hearing the commotion.

"I know where the woman is," Grady said.

B.T. smiled, looked past Grady for Carl then grunted as if he wasn't surprised at his absence. "Come into my office."

He turned and Grady followed before shutting the door behind him.

*****

Nick was preoccupied on the way to town and the work of herding the horses kept him quiet.

Lillian noted how quiet he was, but didn't disturb him by trying to make conversation. Instead she enjoyed watching him work, watching the horses and the scenery.

Finally he spoke.

"Lillian, when we get to town, you can go on over to your dress shop and look it over while I take care of this deal. I'll be over when it's done."

Puzzled, she looked at him.

Why is he suddenly thinking it is fine now to go to my dress shop when it wasn't before? Is he that preoccupied with his horse trading that he's forgotten he didn't think it was safe before?

Well she wasn't going to ask him. She really did need to check on her shop.

Townsfolk stopped to watch as Nick drove the horses through town toward the corral. Thunder rolled as rainclouds darkened the sky. No one appeared to notice Lillian walking quietly down the back of town toward her dress shop, holding the gun down by her side as she hoped the folds of her dress would hide it. Two chickens ran across in front of her, away from the noise and the horses and Lillian froze hoping no one would see her.

But she saw no movement and no one called her name so she began walking again, picking her way around horse droppings.

Lillian wished she had shoes. With any luck, she'd have a pair once she reached the shop. Luck was with her so far.

It was such a relief to see her dress shop was still standing. There was no telling what the angry townsfolk would have done once she was gone and it had been one of her fears that they'd burn the shop down.

They likely believed she'd run off to join her fiancé with the stolen gold when her shop appeared abandoned and no one had seen her.

The question remained whether they'd stolen everything of value with the store being empty for days.

The back door was broken and leaned against the side of the shop. No one had bothered to close it. Lillian stepped inside, walked into the center of the room and stood surveying the damage. Her shoulders slumped.

This had been her new home and she'd settled in, making it hers. She'd taken pride in each detail and in the room upstairs where she lived. She'd worked so hard to make everything just as she'd wanted it. She had loved her little store, the dresses she made, being a part of the town. She'd taken pride in being a storeowner.

She stood looking around her at everything she had worked so hard for. All the lamps were smashed. Paper patterns were torn. Broken glass and paper littered the floor. Dressmaker's dummies were ripped and one had a pair of scissors sticking out of its chest. Stuffing from the dummies was all over. Ribbons and buttons and lace were everywhere.

The two standing mirrors they'd toppled over, shattering on the floor. The third mirror, mounted on the wall, was only cracked.

They had been gifts that Mr. Thomas Shelton had shipped in for her, and one had been installed on the wall. She'd been so grateful to him for the gifts. So much in love.

He had showered her with gifts and she had mistaken that for love.

It had seemed as if he truly cared for her. Particularly as he seemed to be careful with his money at all other times. His bursts of generosity now seemed more as if he had tried to buy her. Not long after she'd accepted the gifts he had attempted to tell her how to run her business. It was the only subject they had ever disagreed upon.

His words came back to her again along with the bitter memory.

"My dear, you have no idea how the gold fever has struck men in these parts. They hear of a gold rush and lose all sense of decency. It isn't safe to keep your gold here when you can come down the street and exchange it for bank notes." He'd closed his hand over hers then said, "I worry about you alone above that store."

Oh, how sincere his expression had been.

She had believed him.

Then he'd gone on to say. "Much as I love to see you walking through the doors of my bank, it would be so much easier for you if you'd simply tell the townsfolk our bank notes are the only currency you will accept. They are new to the concept and not all of them have understood how much safer the notes are."

It had been the sticking point, which she would not agree to. Because no one else had a rule they would only accept the local bank notes. Why would she limit herself in that way?

It had made no sense at the time, but of course now it all made perfect sense.

He was a manipulative man and a scoundrel.

She'd made one mistake after another ever since she packed her bags to come west. One thing she had done right was to listen to her own reasoning in this matter and not to his. She'd hidden a small bag of gold upstairs in her living quarters.

If only it were still there.

She headed up the stairs to look and paused at the top. All her things were gone. Dresses, shoes, combs and her trunk. The room was emptied of everything but the bed and washstand. It looked as if she had never been there, never lived in this space. Not a trace of her remained.

She walked over to the bed, laid the gun down on it and then pulled loose the round wooden knob on the headboard. Inside was a hollow hidey-hole, which had been her grandmother's name for the secret hiding place.

It was there. They hadn't found it.

She exhaled a breath she hadn't even known she held. Then she removed the small bag of gold and tucked it inside her dress. She had just begun to wonder what to do about shoes when she heard a shot.

Nick.

She picked up the gun she'd laid on the bed, turned and raced barefoot down the stairs and out the door.

*****

Nick was working at driving the last of the horses in to the corral when he sensed something was off. Townsfolk who'd been curiously watching had begun to clear the street. From side-glances he noted there wasn't a woman or child in sight.

Another side-glance showed him three men off to the right, by the mercantile, watching him.

A glance to the left. Three more in front of the saloon. One was B.T.

Men with nothing better to do than watch him herd the horses. Men that hadn't been in sight when he'd first ridden into town. Men with hats pulled low enough he couldn't see their eyes.

There was a bad feeling in the pit of his stomach. His gut was clanging the warning bell. He had learned to trust his gut whenever that feeling started in. His trigger finger began to itch.

The last horse was running into the corral when Nick turned his horse around to face B.T. and sat restless on his horse, one hand on his gun, his horse sensing this, also restless beneath him.

He and B.T. watched each other from mistrusting distances.

Nick was the first to speak. "I delivered the horses. Now you deliver the gold."

"I thank you for that." B.T. touched the brim of his bowler hat. "They appear to be mighty fine animals. I do appreciate you bringing them to me."

The nasty smirk on the man standing next to B.T. told Nick all he needed to confirm his suspicion.

"You don't have the gold."

"Why don't you come into the saloon where we can discuss this, like civilized men?"

Civilized men don't string defenseless women up over mine shafts after branding them. Or stand by while other men torture them.

"There's nothing to discuss. You either have the gold or you don't."

"Come now, Mr. Brace. Nick." B.T. flashed a fake smile. "Your woman is the one with the gold. My gold. I want it back." He glanced to one of his men across the street and gestured with his head.

The man moved toward the corral gate to close it.

"Not so fast." Nick drew with his right, his left clicking back the hammer fast.

"Take him." With that B.T. stepped back behind the doors of the saloon.

Nick fired, hitting the man who'd moved to close the gate, just as he caught the movement of a man on his left reaching for his gun and dove from his horse just in time before a bullet whistled over his head.

Leaping to the ground, he fired from underneath his horse and missed, but dove behind a watering trough.

Buffalo Gals was playing on the player piano in the saloon as if there weren't men shooting at Nick from both sides smoke filling the air. The piano kept playing as if it were just another day.

*****

Bullets were flying and smoke filled the air. Lillian was hurrying past the saloon doors when an arm reached out and grabbed her.

B.T. Kingston laughed. "Not so fast."

Lil froze. The gun held down by her side.

If only her skirt hid it. They wouldn't expect her to have a gun.

"Grady," Kingston shouted, "hold up."

Grady and the other gunmen stopped.

Smoke filled the air and it was silent except for one man's cough.

Nick saw her. He shouted. "You okay, Lil?"

"She's fine," Kingston shouted back before she could speak. "She'll continue to be fine if she gives up the gold."

"Let her go," Nick yelled.

Lillian watched Nick as he rose slightly, the urge to come charging in clear by the way his body moved.

She was terrified he would come charging in and be killed. She was terrified of being abused again by these men, but her anger was growing.

They may have scarred her body, but they had not scarred her mind. They had branded her for life, yes. This brand was no longer a mark of their power over her. It was a mark of what she had survived. A mark of how strong she was to have endured.

I am not a victim. I am a survivor.

She had thought those words over and over since her conversation with Nick.

The terror did not take her over this time as it once had. Instead, her anger grew until suddenly she fought. No longer frozen, she twisted and kicked, trying to get away.

Kingston gripped Lil's arm in a tight hold, his fingers digging in.

"You've caused me enough trouble, you stupid bitch." He hissed into her ear. "Now you're going to tell me where that money is."

"Go to hell."

He jammed his gun under her chin. "If I go, I'm taking you with me."

"I'm not afraid of you."

"Kingston let her go," Nick yelled. "She doesn't know where your gold is."

Kingston breathed in her ear. "If you're not afraid for yourself, maybe you should be afraid for your lover."

He turned his gun and as he fired off a shot, Lil elbowed him in the ribs, making his shot go wild, then she kneed him below his belt, making him bend over in pain.

The moment Lil was free she turned to run.

"Oh no you don't."

Still wincing with pain, his hand closed around her ankle and she fell with a thump, dropping the gun she'd held.

As she fell she saw the gun drop and reached for it.

He was pulling her back toward him when her fingers closed over the gun.

She raised it, pulling the hammer back with all she could as she twisted around toward him.

Bang!

Her shot hit him in the forehead.

Blood spewed from the wound and B.T. Kingston dropped on top of Lillian.

Neither of them got up.

"Damn it! Lillian?" Nick called to her as he strained to see her. "You okay?"

She heard him as if from a distance.

His gun poised to shoot, Nick watched her as Grady loomed over Lillian as she looked from the body up at him.

Her torturer. Her tormenter. The leer on his face made her freeze in fear.

Grady kicked Kingston's dead body away, off of her and began to reach for her as she fumbled with the gun, her hands shaking.

"Now you're all mine," he said.

No. No. No.

"And I'll have that gold too."

"Like hell," Nick said.

Grady looked up.

Nick fired.

Grady fell back away from Lil.

Nick turned back to Lil.

She was alive. Alive and holding the gun in her hand, shaking like a leaf, with tears running down her face.

"It's over, Lil."

She looked around slow as if she were taking everything in, in slow motion, the gun hanging from her hand.

"So much blood."

She looked down. It was on her new dress, her hands. The blood stained the white fabric and the violets. The violets.

"My dress."

He held out his hands to her. "Come here, Angel."

She stood shaking.

He took the gun then taking her shaking hands in his, he pulled her to him.

She stepped toward him shakily as he gathered her into his arms.

He held her close, feeling her tremble, glad she was safe.

"The blood," she whispered.

"It will wash away," he said. "We'll clean it off."

"My dress."

"I can buy you ten new dresses."

"My dress was special."

"You are what's special to me Angel. I thought I'd lost you." He held her close. "I thought I'd lost you."

She clung to him without speaking, her eyes closed, she only nodded.

He kissed the top of her head, holding her near. "I'm glad you're okay." He breathed out the tension he'd held in. "So glad."

"I'm glad you're okay, too," she whispered the words so soft against his chest he barely heard her.

"You're going to be all right, Angel. They're gone."

She didn't answer him and he pulled back cupping her chin in his hand, looking deep into her eyes. Seeing the shock of what she'd been through still gripping her, he repeated his words. "You're going to be all right, Angel. It's over."

"It's over," she repeated his words and he could see she was still in shock.

Twice now she'd had to shoot and kill a man. First her cousin, and now B.T. Kingston, the man behind her torture. Lillian was not a killer at heart. The shock had hit her hard.

Killing a man never got easier. Not even when the man was trying to kill you and you had no choice if you wanted to stay alive.

She had been though so much in a short period of time, but finally it was over. She was going to be all right. Relief she would be all right coursed through him and he wanted nothing more than to pull her close and hold her.

What she needed was to be away from the sight of death all around her, to be able to clean up and feel normal again.

He looked at Lillian's dress and seeing the blood stains on it he remembered her talking about the violets and her grandmother. Now that he'd remembered why the dress meant so much to her, he would find her another dress with violets if he had to send all the way to Paris for it.

"Come on, let's get you cleaned up." Taking her hand he led her out and away from the saloon, past the dead bodies and the gawking townsfolk who had decided to emerge from the buildings they'd hidden in.

He noted the way they looked at Lillian. The glares from the men. The judgmental stares of the women. The undercurrent of anger, which ran through the townsfolk toward the slight woman who walked by his side. This delicate woman they thought was a criminal had been through so much and finally found the strength to stand up for herself by shooting the man who was truly the criminal in town.

His hand tightened around hers as he ushered her away from them and the look of warning he sent to them said stay away her. Even their whispering halted beneath that look as he led her back to her shop.

Chapter Eleven

The sheriff was a mousy man who seemed disgruntled over B.T. Kingston's sudden demise. B.T. had paid him to look the other way and the river of money had now dried up. Neither Nick or Lillian were charged with murder even though it was clear to everyone in town that they'd killed B.T. and most of his gang.

The undertaker was busy fitting coffins for all six of the dead men. Townsmen had started sucking down the whiskey in the saloon just as fast as they could, almost as if they were afraid Kingston would return from the grave and charge them for it or call in their markers. There was a lot of ugly talk going around about Lillian.

The townsfolk would not so much as nod at Lillian and other than the sheriff and the undertaker, not one of them had spoken a word to her.

They still suspected her of knowing where her fiancé had hidden the gold. Many felt she'd brought trouble with her when she came to town and they couldn't wait to be rid of her, provided she gave up the gold first.

Nick, ever one to watch and listen, heard the rumblings and he didn't like what he heard.

Lillian could not stay here.

He had to convince her.

"Come north with me. Make a new start." Nick gazed into her eyes. "I want you to see my ranch. The house is small, but it's comfortable."

"I'd like to see it." Lil smiled. "But I can't ride away just yet."

"Why not?'

"I need to sell my store first and it is a mess. I have a lot to do here before I can even think of leaving."

"You could ride away from this town, put it all in the past in the past, right now, if you'd let yourself. Walk away from it all. Come with me."

She frowned, but did not answer, as she looked over toward her store.

So that was her answer. She was clinging to the past, determined to salvage all she could from her shop before she could move on.

She couldn't just go with him. She didn't love him. He'd do his best by her, but it hurt that she didn't love him, couldn't just go with him. He'd hoped for more.

Still, he loved her and would do anything to help her.

"You want to fix up the shop to sell it? That's not a problem, Lillian. I can help you."

She shook her head. "You have other things to do."

"Nothing more important pressing right now. Nothing more important than you."

I knew it the moment I first thought I'd almost lost you.
Nick took her hand in his. "Let me help you, Angel."
"It's such a mess I don't even know where to start."
"All right. Let's go look at it."
They walked to the store, his hand wrapped around hers.

Lillian seemed to only want to focus on business matters, but she was allowing him to hold her hand. Perhaps in time she would allow more than soft kisses and holding hands. He wouldn't rush her. After what she'd been through she would need time.

He would give her all the time she needed.

They paused by the back door.

Before they entered through the broken back door, he stopped to examine it. "That's easily fixed."

"Good." Lillian answered him, but refused to look at him. Inside, Nick surveyed the room then walked up to Lillian and slid his arm around her waist.

*****

Lillian felt the heat from his body warming her. Again, she felt the comfort of his presence in a physical way and she was glad he was there for her.

It was as if he knew she was upset.

Being with Nick felt so right. When she was within his arms it felt like coming home.

She'd better not get used to this, or like it too much.

It would only hurt all the more when he rode away.

She wished he didn't have to go, though she knew he would leave her. She'd already taken up much of his time and now he felt had to stay to help her get back on her feet again. It was better to focus on business things than to think about what he meant to her.

Thinking about that and knowing Nick and I have no future will only hurt. She closed her eyes forcing the thought away. When she opened them again he was watching her with a soft gaze.

"It's not that bad, Angel. Nothing I can't fix."

He pulled her close and kissed the top of her head. She slid her arms around his waist and held onto him, closing her eyes.

"Thank you, Nick," she whispered into his muscled chest.

He must have heard her because he replied. "You're welcome, Angel."

The warmth in his words and the heat his body put out warmed her up inside and she wanted to stay within his embrace. She just wanted to stay here and feel that everything was all right again and this was where she belonged, warm and safe within his arms.

He held her for a few moments longer before pulling back, as if he knew it was what she'd needed. Then he looked down into her eyes with a smile and said. "Guess we have work to do."

"Yes," she sighed. "We'd better get started."

Before I give too much of my heart to you or get to used to how good it feels within your arms.

He gave her a squeeze and then stepped back. "Let's get started. Do you have a broom?"

"I did have. It must be here somewhere."

"Well, if you don't find it, we'll buy a new one. I'll need a few tools."

She found the broom in a corner. "Here it is."

"All right. You sweep and I'll move the larger things. If you can start in this corner we can pile anything you want to keep over there until the repairs are done."

There were things she could salvage. She would have to sort out the ribbons and buttons and fabric and save everything she could. She nodded at him and taking the broom, started in.

There was so much to be done.

It felt good to have a plan. It gave her something to focus on beyond the destruction and what they had done to her.

"We'll clear away the rubbish and then head over to the mercantile to pick up the things we'll be needing."

"That sounds like a good idea. Thank you, Nick."

"You're welcome, Angel." He smiled at her. "I like helping you. It brings me pleasure."

He brought her all sorts of pleasure too. The kind that made her blush just thinking about it. She focused her mind back on her tasks and tried not to think of that right now.

It took all morning just getting the floor cleaned up so they could walk through without stepping on glass and shards of mirror.

They walked over to the mercantile. Mr. Brown had been rather upset when she opened her shop, as it had been in competition with him to sell dresses. Even though he'd settled down when he learned she would purchase her sewing supplies from him, he still viewed her as a threat.

So it came as no surprise to her when he said, "I'm surprised you're planning to fix the shop. It's not likely you'll find anyone to help you."

"She has all the help she needs," Nick spoke up. "I'll just pay for these tools and we'll be going."

"I'm only fixing up the shop to sell. If you hear of anyone who would like to buy it please let me know."

The man only grunted as he tallied up what Nick owed him. It was obvious he could care less.

"Lillian, if you could wait over by the door, I'd like to have a word with Mr. Brown."

She nodded and moved over to the door.

Nick spoke in hushed tones to the man then purchased the tools and fixings for their lunch and they went back to her store.

They sat upon the floor in a cleared space to eat.

"Most of the fabrics are salvageable, and all the ribbons and buttons once I wash off the mud they tracked in."

"See, it wasn't as bad as you thought. I'm sure you'll be back to making pretty things before you know it. Do you want to continue selling your dresses? In another town? "

"I'm not sure. I wasn't all that successful at it. I really haven't thought beyond salvaging what I can and selling the shop. The women in town are never going to buy dresses from me. I see the way they look at me now. Everyone hates me. But even before that very few of them bought my dresses."

"Lillian, women here have a harder life than the women back east. Most of them make their own clothes."

"Yes, I learned that the hard way." She ran her hand over the fabric. "No, I don't see me owning a dress shop as long as I am living out west."

"Is it what you want to do? Is owning a dress shop your dream?"

"It used to be."

Now I dream of you.

He nodded. "Sometimes dreams can change. But from what I've seen here, you have quite the touch with a needle."

"I don't want to go back east." She was aware of the brand beneath her dress. "Living here has changed me. I'm not the same woman I used to be."

He came over and took her in his arms. "I like the woman you have become. I like her very much."

She looked up into his eyes and saw the respect and admiration there. She saw tenderness and caring. And she knew that in his arms was the place she wanted to be, wherever that was.

"I would like to show you my ranch, my lifestyle. See what you think of it."

"Yes, I'd like that very much."

"Maybe you would take to ranching if you gave it a try."

"Maybe I would."

"I could teach you."

"Yes, you could."

He bent down and kissed her lips softly then pulled away again.

"Angel, it's tempting to stay here kissing you and forget about all this work."

"Mmm, yes, I could forget too."

This was the first he'd hinted at any sort of future for them. She was afraid to hope for more than this.

Still her hopes and her dreams were taking flight, completely ignoring the sensible practicalities. Hope that she could lose her past by leaving it behind her and starting over somewhere else. Dreams of what their life could be like if they were together. Threaded through all that was the simple fact that she loved him.

A simple fact that would not be denied, whatever she chose to do.

"The sooner we're done with this, the sooner I can take you to my ranch."

"Yes," she sighed, "true."

He ran his finger across her lip. "I plan to pick up this evening where we left off."

"Oh, I hope you do."

He stepped away with a wink, chuckled and moved over to the remaining mirror. "Wouldn't take much for this one to break by the look of it. Someone hit it with something hard to make it crack. These cracks are just going to keep getting bigger. It should come down."

"Yes, take it down. No one is going to want to put a dress shop in here again. Not when this one wasn't successful. I am just hoping someone buys the building." She began rolling up the fabrics neatly.

"Someone will. If you advertise it in the eastern papers, you'll have all sorts of offers."

Nick was pulling pieces of mirror away from the wall.

"I wonder if Mr. Brown would consider purchasing this fabric from me?"

"You can always ask."

"He barely speaks to me. But it's worth a try. I'm not going to keep all this fabric. There's too much to carry on a horse."

Nick didn't answer. He was sitting back on his heels, frowning at the wall, where he'd removed the mirror.

"Nick, what is it?"

"Lil, do you know why there would be a panel behind this mirror?"

"No." She frowned and came over to stand beside him. "It wasn't there before my fiancé installed the mirror. It was just a wall."

"I'm going to take it out."

"All right."

Nick pulled the nails out with the hammer and she stood back watching him work.

He removed the section of wood. Behind it was a hole.

"Lil," Nick sucked in a breath. "You need to look at this."

She stepped close and peered in and gasped.

Inside the hole were two bags of gold.

He'd hidden some of the gold here. Kingston and Carl had been right. They just hadn't looked hard enough.

She turned and flew into Nick's arms. "You found it! You found the gold!"

"We found it, Angel." Nick wrapped his arms around her, smiling at her happiness and excitement.

She'd looked like an angel to him before, but now she had a glow about her. He wished he could see her this happy every day. See that glow in her eyes and on her face.

"Oh, I just can't believe it! It was here all along. How did he do it?" Her eyes widened. "Oh. That's why he wanted me to open my shop. He wanted to get the gold before he left town." She shook her head. "I couldn't do it because I having dinner out at the Marstons' ranch. Her daughter was having the final fitting for her wedding gown and I had to be there. He came out to get me but I couldn't leave and he got mad and stormed off."

"I'm surprised he didn't break in and take it."

"Carl said he'd been hanging around my shop acting strange. He probably would have, if Carl hadn't been watching him."

Nick looked back at the hole. "This can't be all of the gold, if he was doing this as long as you said. That much gold is too heavy to take all at once. He must have stored the rest of it elsewhere, what he couldn't take with him." His eyebrows rose. "Two bags. That's still a lot of gold. What are you going to do with it?"

"Oh, Nick. It isn't mine. I can't keep it. Oh!" Her hands flew to her mouth and her eyes widened.

"What is it, Angel?"

She dropped her hands away. "I have to give it back to all those people he stole it from."

Nick looked at her in surprise. "Now why that should surprise me, I don't know. It's the sort of thing you would do."

"The gold is not all here, but I imagine what is here will help the ones that are hurting."

"Yes, it probably would."

"That's what I'll do. Everyone who had deposits will get back a portion of what they lost." Her eyes shone with tears. "Oh, Nick, some of them are really hurting."

He gathered her into his arms and said, "Lillian, you are the most amazing woman. I always knew you were an angel."

She smiled and laughed. Fully laughed for the first time since he'd met her. He watched the joy in her face, the kind of joy, which came from giving, and he knew she was the only woman for him.

He wanted to spend the rest of his life finding ways to make her smile, seeing that joy upon her face. His smile grew deeper as he thought of the information he'd obtained from Mr. Brown.

All Nick had to do was contact the company that had shipped the dress with the violets on it to Mr. Brown's store and he now had the information to do it.

For now it was a secret. She would be so surprised when she saw it. He couldn't wait to see the look on her face.

He hoped to spend the rest of his life finding ways to surprise her and make her happy.

*****

Nick, being more of a realist than Lillian, was nearby with his gun handy as she attempted to repay some of the townsfolk their money. He watched as person after person took the gold Lillian offered, yet offered her no forgiveness. By the time she'd run through the first bag of gold, he was fed up with the way they spoke to her and the way they looked at her. Enough was enough.

He interrupted. "Lillian, excuse me, darlin', but it is time we go now." He fingered his gun watching the townsfolk. "It's a long ride back to my place."

"Oh, well, I wasn't quite done."

"Yes," he interrupted her again. "You are. You've done enough." He nodded toward the townsfolk. "Too bad most of them don't appreciate what you've done here today."

"I'm just trying to do the right thing."

"I know angel, and I love you all the more for it. But it's time to go now. Let me take you home with me, away from this town. You don't belong here."

She looked out at the faces looking back at her and realized he was right. She didn't belong here. Never had. She belonged in the warmth of his arms. Home, wherever that was, was where Nick was.

He was right. It was time to go. She felt bad about not telling them about the second bag of gold, but they had treated her so ugly even when she'd given out the first one. And much had been stolen from her too. Much more than gold. Nick was right. It was time to walk away from this.

"Gather your things. I'll get the horses."

Nick would be herding all but a few of the horses back home where he would wait for another buyer.

Lillian hurried back to her shop, his words ringing through her head.

He'd said he loved her. Almost as if it had slipped out, but still he'd said it.

Her hope took flight.

She could pack her personal things quick. What there was left of them after they'd stolen everything but the unfinished dresses in her shop. They'd taken her personal things. It wouldn't take long to pack just two dresses she still needed to hem and a nightgown.

Hurrying to throw them into her travel bag as she waited for him, she thought over what he'd said.

He loves me all the more. Though he'd never told her he loved her, every action he had taken took spoke the words for him.

What if he, like her, held back from saying the words, afraid everything would vanish into smoke if they were spoken?

When he came back to the shop for her, she watched him closely.

He seemed anxious to leave as he glanced about the shop.

Who knew how many days he had lost from taking care of her and what condition his ranch might be in after he'd been away so long? She knew nothing of ranching and hoped the delay hadn't caused him more problems.

She wanted to be a help to him, not a burden. Perhaps there were things she could do to help him with the ranch.

When his gaze landed on her after sweeping the room, she looked back into his warm brown eyes and smiled.

"I'm ready if you are," she said.

"You haven't packed your dress making things yet. Is this all you're taking?"

"Yes. Mr. Brown didn't want to purchase any of this," she swept her arm, taking in the contents of her shop. "But there's no reason to take it with me. I am done with shop keeping. I will put an ad in the eastern newspapers for the sale of the shop and that can be handled from wherever I move to."

"And where would you like to move to?"

Did he not realize she wanted to be with him? He watched her waiting for her answer.

"I'm ready to learn to live on a ranch. There's nothing here for me and I have no desire to go back east."

"I was hoping you'd say that. This is no place for you. But are you sure you have everything packed that you need?"

She stepped closer resting her hands on his chest, looking up into his eyes. "I have everything I need and want right here. If you still want me to come with you, there's nowhere else I'd rather be."

The warmth in his eyes and the way his arms wrapped around her gave her the answer she sought; yet still she longed to hear the words.

"Angel, I was afraid you wouldn't come with me and I didn't want to lose you. But it had to be your choice. Are you sure?"

"I feel safe in your arms, as if it is where I belong."

"I'm glad."

"You are my home. Yes, I am sure."

"I thought I'd lost you in that gunfight. Those were the worst moments of my life." His eyes searched hers, telling her, yet still he hadn't said the words. "Three times now I've thought I'd lose you. This last time was the worst. I never want to lose you Angel."

He was saying everything but those three little words.

So she spoke them softly. "I love you Nick."

She felt his chest expand as he pulled her even closer. "Lillian I've loved you from the moment I saw you. You are a gift dropped into my life, like an angel dropped down from the sky. Didn't you wonder why I call you Angel?"

She shook her head and smiled.

"I fell in love with you before I even knew your name."

Lillian felt her heart expand as tears of joy welled up and spilled from her eyes and laughter bubbled up.

"No, I didn't know."

He kissed her and she closed her eyes, losing all sense of time and place as the kiss, which began so softly, deepened.

They kissed for the longest time.

And when they finally rode away from her shop, she rode away without looking back.

The End

Made in the USA
Charleston, SC
29 May 2013

About Debra Parmley

Debra Parmley is the author of two western historical romance, Dangerous Ties and A Desperate Journey; one contemporary ro[m] Aboard the Wishing Star, and one 1920's historical romance, Trappi[ng] Butterfly. For more about Debra's books as well as her poetry and stories please visit her website. http://www.debraparmley.com

Originally from Ohio, Debra now lives in Tennessee, just o[utside] Memphis. She is married to her high school sweetheart and has tw[o.] Debra enjoys history and in her spare time is a living history re-e[nactor] with the Society for Creative Anachronism where she enjoys pri[mitive] archery, embroidery and dance.

It is with infinite love and gratitude that she gives thanks fo[r the] opportunity to fulfill her dream of sharing her stories with readers al[l over] the world. One of Debra's greatest joys is hearing from her readers.